THE TENEBROUS HARE

by
M. J. Marks

PublishAmerica

Baltimore

First printing

ISBN: 1-4137-1673-3
PUBLISHED BY PUBLISHAMERICA, LLLP
www.publishamerica.com
Baltimore

Printed in the United States of America

This is the word of the Lord to Zerubbabel:
"Not by might nor by power, but by my
Spirit," says the Lord Almighty.
Zechariah 4:6

THE

TENEBROUS

HARE

Long fingers that had seen many years of hard labor painstakingly secured the red, white and blue handmade quilt around the six-year-old boy who lay in bed. The child's eyelids were heavy with sleep, but he fought it as he looked up with admiration and love in his eyes. He observed his grandfather who stooped over him, adjusting the quilt neatly around his neck. He loved his grandfather, even though he was old and could no longer do many physical things with him. However that didn't bother him, he loved having his grandfather around.

He could not recall seeing his grandparents very often because they lived far away and grandmother was sick quite often. Several months ago his parents explained to him that grandmother went to heaven to be an angel, and grandfather was coming to live with them. He didn't understand about going to heaven and being an angel, but he liked the idea that his grandfather was going to live with them.

He always wanted to have his very own grandfather. Billy, at school was always talking about his grandfather and all the wonderful things they did together. Grandfather couldn't do all the things Billy's grandfather did, but he would come to school almost every day just to be with him. When his class went on field trips or had special guests, Grandfather would come. The kids loved having him around. He didn't mind sharing him at school because when they went home, grandfather was all his.

There were times when Grandfather felt sad because he missed Grandmother. Tears would surface in his eyes and run down his cheeks. He too missed Grandmother, even though he could not remember what she looked like. Grandfather had pictures of her in his room, but her face didn't trigger any memory.

When grandfather was sad, he would give him a big hug and tells him how much he liked living with them. Grandfather would smile and say that being with him made some of the pain go away.

Once the quilt was exactly right, he planted a light kiss on his grandson's forehead. Gently, he swept the hair back from his forehead with hands that were wrinkled and loving. He sighed, content to be at his grandson's bedside.

He looked so much like his son when he was his age. Just looking at him brought back pleasurable memories. He missed the days when they would hold hands, content in each other's presence. They had fun playing silly games and laughing until their stomachs ached. Watching the minnows swim back and forth and skipping rocks across the lake near their home, were some of their favorite activities. On warm sunny days, they would lie in the grass, watching the clouds roll by; naming each formation. Those were special times, but now his son was grown with a family of his own. It was sad that his son's job kept him away from home several days at a time, leaving a void in his young son's life. A void he was happy to be able to fill.

All responsibilities had fallen on his daughter-in-law's shoulders as she tried to be mother and father. In the fourth month of her pregnancy it was impossible for her to do many things. Within seven months of the pregnancy complications arose and the doctor put her on bed rest until the baby was born. With such restrictions, she was unable to do any household chores. Now the responsibilities fell on him. He did the cooking, cleaning, and keeping up with his energetic grandson, something he was happy to do. Doing the daily household chores kept him busy and he no longer had time to sit, think and feel lonely about his wife. He loved his wife and they had had a wonderful life together, but now he knows she is out of pain and much happier.

He sighed, being old was not as awful as he once thought. Not as long as he was around his family. They give him more joy than he thought was ever possible.

"Grandfather, read me a story," his grandson said sitting up, dislodging the carefully placed quilt. Without waiting for a reply, he reached over to the bedside table and grasped his favorite book, *The Little Red Fire Engine.* He knew the story by heart, but he loved hearing his grandfather read to him because he would make funny sounds while reading the book.

"First, you must lie down," Grandfather said smiling.

"Okay, grandfather," he said allowing him to readjust the quilt around his small shoulders.

"Read me the red book? Okay?"

Taking the book from the child's small hands, he bent over and picked up the other books that had fallen to the floor, in his grandson's haste to retrieve his favorite book. He looked at the title, but the words would not focus clearly. Lately, he had noticed that he was unable to focus clearly when he tried to read. He knew he should call to make an appointment to get his eyes checked, but his pride prevented him from making the call. He knew he was getting older but to begin wearing glasses at seventy-two years old was a blow to his pride.

Blinking his eyes, he tried again to focus, but the words remained blurred.

"Well son," he said taking a deep breath. "My eyes have been giving me trouble and I can't see as well as I use to," he said laying the book on the table with the others.

"Oh," the young boy said with sadness in his eyes. He didn't want his grandfather to get old. It just wasn't fair.

Grandfather saw the hurt and sadness in his eyes. Thinking quickly, he spoke, "I may not be able to read you a story tonight, but I can tell you one that my father told me years ago about a hare and tortoise."

"I know that story, grandfather," he said, feeling disappointed. "Tell me another one. Pleeeassse."

"Oh," grandfather said with glee in his tired eyes. "You have not heard the one I am going to tell you. No, son, this story is an original."

"What's an o-rig-i-nal, Grandfather?" the young boy asked sounding out the word.

"It means that it's the only one of its kind and its' very special."

"Really, Grandfather!" he said sitting up with excitement in his eyes. "How come this one is an o-rig-i-nal?"

"Because this story tells about the courage of a small tortoise who would not allow his smallness, or difference defeat him," he said urging his grandson to lie back down.

"Really?" he said as excitement danced in his eyes.

"Yep," Grandfather said as his heart jumped with glee.

"Grandfather, I would love to hear the o-rig-i-nal story!" he exclaimed settling deeply beneath the covers.

Grandfather smiled as he walked over and retrieved an old rocking chair that was stationed against the window. Pulling the chair near the bed, he settled his tired body into it. Running his hands over the arms of the chair, brought back many wonderful memories.

7

Oh God, he said to himself as he ran his hands over the arms of the chair. They were smoothed and worn in several places and carved in one the arms was the date *June 10, 1872.* That was the year his grandfather bought the chair for his first child.

His grandfather felt pride and admiration as he related how the chair became a part of their history. He was twenty-two when he met the most beautiful woman in the world. Grandmother had only been in America for two weeks when he met her at the clothing factory where he worked. At the age of sixteen, she had come across the ocean from Poland to America alone to live with her older brother and family. It was love at first sight

Wanting to please his wife, he worked odd jobs and saved every penny. The day before their first child came home from the hospital, he went out and purchased the rocking chair. It was very expensive but it was worth every penny to see the excitement in his wife's eyes. She began to cry uncontrollably when she saw the chair. His heart sank to his knees as she rushed from the room sobbing. He thought he was doing a good deed. Two weeks later they were married.

When his wife became pregnant, she was depressed and longed to have her mother by her side to help with the baby. but instead he had made his wife sad. A few minutes later she returned with a picture in her hand. He didn't understand what was going on until he looked at the picture. The rocking chair he purchased was an exact replica of the one in the picture her mother was sitting in.

Since that day the rocking chair had been passed down through grandfather's five children and then the grandchildren. His aunts and uncles married and relocated to other states, except his father. None of them wanted the rocking chair except his father. When he married and his wife became pregnant, his father gave him the rocking chair and it had remained with him until his first grandchild was born.

They had dreamed of having four children but after giving birth to their son, she was left weak and her mobility became limited. The doctors could not find any reason for her illness. Out of desperation, he took her to a specialist and it was discovered that she had a tumor which kept her from bearing any more children.

Thirty years later she went to the doctor because of bleeding and it was detected that cancer had invaded her body. There was nothing they could do for her. He took her home and took care of her until she died a few months later. In the last few weeks of her life, she was in great pain and confined to her bed. Sometimes the pain was so severe that she would cling to him with all her strength, as the tears flowed down her face. The memories brought a deep pain to his heart.

"Grandfather?"

The voice brought him back to the present as he gripped the arms of the chair. He missed this old chair. For hours he would sit in this chair reading bedtime stories to his son or just rocking him to sleep.

"Grandfather," his grandson spoke again. He saw the lost look in grandfather's eyes and knew he was thinking about grandmother, and he felt a sadness that gripped his heart. He wished he could make the pain go away.

"Yes?" Grandfather said as he blinked the one lone tear that escaped the corner of his eye. He looked at his grandson and saw the sadness in his eyes. *Now was not the time to think painful thoughts*, he said to himself as he wiped the tear away with the back of his hand.

"Yes?" he repeated.

"Are you going to tell me the o-rig-i-nal story?"

He smiled.

"Yes, I will tell you the original story about a brave little tortoise who faces many obstacles and becomes a hero."

In a land far, far away from the hustle and bustle of humans; deep in the heart of a green meadow lived a kingdom of animals ruled by a hare named Saul. From all appearances, Saul looked like any ordinary hare, however he frequently displayed very unusual and bizarre behavior. Frightened of what he may do to them, they avoided him and whispered behind his back.

The animals' sole desire was that Saul would have the same personality as his father King John.

King John was a cheerful hare that adored dressing in bright colorful clothes, eating and attending many parties. The royal family habit included giving or attending parties.

No one in the entire kingdom could host a party like the Queen, especially when it was the king's birthday. For two memorable weeks, the animals celebrated. The Queen's guest-list consisted of hundreds of dignitaries who came from all the surrounding kingdoms. Beautiful decorative coaches lined up for miles awaiting their turn to disembark their owners. The coaches were decorated in arrays of expensive and elaborate decorations both outside and inside. The padded seats were covered with rich velvet or imported silks. The guests were so numerous that tents had to be erected to accommodate them.

Weeks before the king's birthday, the staff worked around the clock to ensure that everything went perfectly. Large colorful lights that could be seen for miles away were strung around the castle, and large banners wishing the king a happy birthday, were hung in front of the castle. For the weeks of festivities, delicacies from around the world were shipped in, along with fine silks and leather to dress the royal family.

A week before the king's birthday, the animals would line up on main street as the royal dignitaries, dressed in their finery, would parade before them. The procession would start at mid-morning and ran late into the evening. The animals didn't mind because all year they had been waiting for this particular day. They looked forward to it because, at the end of the parade, was their beloved king sitting high upon his throne. Along with the king were carts fill with candy, toys and treats for the children and boxes of fruit and vegetables for the adults. After the parade of dignitaries passed, the entertainment would commence. The entertainment consisted of several outdoor shows, magicians, clowns and rides for the children.

The gifts for the king numbered in the thousands and had to be housed in rooms off the throne room. The brightly colored boxes contained costly jewelry, gold, silver, crystal, fine leather, candy, spices, books and colorful and elaborate fabrics from all over the world.

Once the festivities were over and the guests had packed up their belongings and left the kingdom, the animals breathed a sigh of relief because the kingdom would return to normal for another year.

The following day the king would recline on a bed of soft pillows surrounded by his wife and daughters. One by one, the staff would gather up the gifts and present them to him. The ordeal was tedious as it took days to open and present the gifts to the king. Like children the royal family would *ooh* and *ahh* as each gift was displayed. Once the gifts were viewed, cataloged and thank-you letters sent out, it was the servants' responsibility to find space in rooms that were already crammed with gifts from previous years.

King John was greatly respected by all the animals as a fair and just ruler. In those days there were no jails or prisons because the king didn't have the heart to punish anyone. It was a time that all the animals were happy.

Even though the king was admired and loved by the animals, he had one shortcoming, he loved to eat, and eat he did. He rarely walked and when he did he had to stop every few steps just to catch his breath.

It was the duty of sixteen strong soldiers to transport him from one place to another seated on his royal throne. Because of the king's great bulk, the poles supporting the throne were made from the strongest wood in the forest. Each year two soldiers had to be added to accommodate the king's added weight. Not only was the king overweight but also his wife and three daughters. They did not exercise and loved to eat rich food and had a passion for sweets, just as he did.

Saul, the eldest child, did not embrace his family's taste for rich and spicy food and the lack of physical exercise. At a young age, he made up his mind to be different from his family. He wanted the animals to admire and worship him because he would be their king one day. Each morning he would rise before the sun peaked over the horizon, and before the animals had risen to began their morning chores, and run for five miles. After his run, he would return to the castle and exercise in his room for another hour.

The king and his family considered him an eccentric and egotistic maniac. If he wasn't exercising or picking at his food, he would be in his room reading. Several times his father tried, unsuccessfully, to persuade him to abandon such foolishness. Saul held a strong belief that a strong body and a knowledgeable mind were the key to success.

Two things the king detested about his son's habit were his reluctance in attending parties and showing no interest in any of the females that attended the parties. While the parties were commencing, Saul would be in his room with his head buried in a book.

At the age of twelve, King John was so disgruntled with his son's strange behavior and disposition that he sent him to live with his uncle. He had hoped that his brother would be able to persuade his son to change his peculiar habits. After living ten years with his uncle, Saul returned home. His father was amazed at the changes in his son. Not only was he a head and shoulder taller than all the hares in the land, but he was muscular and quite handsome. The young women admired his beauty, however Saul did not embrace their admiration. His father was dismayed. He had hoped that his son would have changed his ways.

Unknown to King John, Saul's perception of the young women was the same as the one of his mother and sisters, whose attitudes he abhorred.

Undeterred King John ordered his son to attend the parties and introduced him to every eligible young hare of notable breeding. Saul fulfilled his duties by dancing and talking to the young women at the parties but he never showed favoritism to any of them. When the young female hares would come to visit, he would sneak out of the castle and stay away for days at a time. His behavior infuriated the king but he was powerless in controlling his son's behavior.

The king had announced to his son and all the animals that in a month he would reveal whom his son would be united in marriage to. Saul tried to persuade his father not to choose a bride for him, but his father refused to listen to any more of his excuses.

On the eve of the announcement King John, his family, seven young potential brides and over eighty guests were sitting at the table eating the evening meal.

The king was dressed in a bright yellow suit with ten gold buttons down the front and matching pants that came above his massive calves and he wore yellow leather shoes with gold buckles to match. His wife and daughters also were dressed in bright yellow dresses with tiny gold buttons down the front and yellow slippers. The king was happy. The bride whom he had chosen for his son would be arriving the next day for the festivities.

The king was in a festive mood even though his son refused to wear the suit of clothes he had made for him. Instead he sat at the table with a long face, dressed in a green shirt and pants, rarely talking to anyone.

King John had tried many schemes to persuade his son to be more sociable, but he would only remind him of his extravagant spending and outlandish choice of clothes. The king felt that his son would not make a very good king, he was too tense and took life too seriously.

When the king become frustrated, he would eat and eat. Tonight was no exception. While he was eating his third piece of apple pie, he grabbed at his chest and slumped in his chair. Within an hour, the beloved king was dead.

With the king's death also went the bride he had chosen for his son. He was so secretive, he didn't even tell his wife. Saul was sad but joyous at the same time. He did not want to marry anyone until he was ready to marry. He informed the seven young hares and family that there was not going to be a wedding.

This was a sad time for the animals as they grieved the passing of their beloved king. In their grief all the windows and doors were covered with black bows and wreaths. Friends and family came from miles away to mourn the passing of King John. There were so many animals in attendance that it took four days for everyone to parade past his coffin.

As the body lay in state the weather was foul and the sky was cloudy and overcast. On the last day the sky opened and it rained. The animals felt that even nature mourned the passing of their beloved king. Yes this was a say day for the animals.

The next day after the king was buried, preparation began for Saul's inauguration. The animals remained after the funeral to witness the carnation of the new king. They knew from the past, that the king's family would have a royal celebration to celebrate the inauguration of the new king.

Saul's mother was grieved at the passing of her husband, but duty called and she began preparing for the elaborate celebration. When words reached Saul's ear about what his mother had planned for his inauguration, he was furious! He canceled all the orders his mother had placed with the merchants and put them out of the castle.

His mother was outraged when she learned that her son had canceled everything she had planned. She sought an audience with her son, but he refused to see her. She was so angry and embarrassed by her son's behavior that she locked herself in her room. Saul didn't care about his mother's temper tantrums. Over the years he had learned to ignore them. He was not his father and he would not allow her to rule him the way she had ruled his father.

The animals were disappointed when they realized that there was not going to be elaborate food, dancing and merriment, so they hastily gathered their belongings and left the castle. By the time Saul was crowned king, there were only a handful of spectators left. The ceremony was simple, lasting only ten minutes. It was a disappointing day. The animals knew without a doubt that Saul was not like his father.

Immediately after Saul's inauguration, he summoned the secretary and treasurer inquiring about the financial state of the kingdom. He was struck speechless, as the nervous secretary reported that the kingdom was penniless and heavily in debt. The royal family was spending twice the amount of money that was collected from taxes each year on entertainment and personal usage. The amount of expenses his mother indulged on the king's funeral was the whole year's budget, money that the kingdom was unable to repay.

Saul made many changes, starting with the staff in the castle. He dismissed half the staff employed in the castle. When invitations came in from the surrounding towns to attend parties, he refused them.

His mother was outraged about her son's changes and the restrictions he put upon the castle and her family. They were unable to purchase new clothes, no money was allotted for parties and they had to take care of only their personal needs. She ranted, raved and cried for days trying to persuade her son to allow her and her daughters the privilege of purchasing new clothes and shoes and having their own personal maids to wait upon them.

Saul's changes did not affect the animals in the town, but only his own household.

The animals were relieved as they fell into a natural routine under the Saul's leadership until the Summer of Celebration arrived.

Traditionally, each year on the first day of summer, all the animals in the forest would came together to celebrate this great day with a grand parade consisting of floats, bands and clowns. Afterward there were more celebrations consisting of games, dancing and lots of socializing.

The origin of the celebration began years ago when king John's great-grandfather planted an oak seed commencing the beginning of the yearly celebration. Special care went into the maintenance and nurturing of the tree, and over the years it became the biggest, tallest and oldest oak tree in the forest. It had enormous branches that spanned outward and upward toward heaven. Beneath the tree, the ground was kept bare of any vegetation and the ground was hard from the many celebrations. On the outskirts of the circle, luscious green shrubs, flowers and bushes grew. By the time the celebration, arrived the colorful flowers were at their peak, emitting a sweet odor that attracted many pollen insects.

All year the animals looked forward to the annual celebration and went through elaborate preparation in designing their floats and uniforms. Their time together consisted of laughter and gaiety, carefree and free of spirit as they enjoyed themselves. This gave them the opportunity to socialize with animals they hadn't seen since the previous year.

On the day of the celebration, the day was always hot and the sky cloudless. Some of the animals had worked many days and long hours to ensure that this was the grandest day of the year.

The festivities always commenced with a lively and colorful parade through town which began at the Town Hall building. It was the largest building in town painted bright red, the mayor's favorite color. The first level was where the animals brought their taxes and took care of all their legal matters. The second floor was where the mayor and his family lived.

Years ago Thomas D. Badger decided that the town needed a mayor, so he elected himself. Next he decided that the town needed a building to symbolize his status and Town Hall was built. Over the years the town had accepted that the Badger family would live in the building and that he would automatically become the mayor.

Samuel Badger had been the mayor for twenty-five years after his father retired. He was loved, admired and respected by the citizens, but they did not take him seriously.

On the day of the festival the animals lined both sides of Main Street and those in the parade got into formation. As a tradition, the mayor and his family always led the parade dressed in their traditional dress of red and white.

Mayor Badger was a short, barrel-chested and wore wire-rimmed glasses. He didn't need the glasses but he thought it made him look more distinguished. His hair was slicked back from his face and parted down the middle, accentuating his small eyes and his thick mustache. While the mayor was short and rounded, his wife was tall and slim. They both dressed in similar suits of red pants, jacket and white shirt. The wife always looked striking in her outfit, but the mayor's suit was a different story. The mayor's suit was over five years old and he had put on considerable weight. His wife had tried unsuccessfully to persuade him to loose weight, but the mayor insisted that he had gained only a few pounds and he had at least five more years of wear left in the suit. The suit was tight, so tight, that every seam was stretched to its limit. It was a wonder that he ever managed to get into the pants. The animals would watch just to see if he could sit down without the pants ripping. The pants were so tight around his waist that he had to use two safety pins and a belt just to keep them fastened. The jacket was another story. It no longer fit and one would have thought it was his son's jacket. The sleeves rose a third up his arms, barring his beefy arms. He had not been unable to fasten the buttons for years, but that never deterred him. Everyone thought he looked ridiculous in his outfit, except for the mayor. He stood proudly with his family with a bright smile on his face.

The mayor's children took after their mother in size and stature, were dressed in red shorts, vests and white shirt. They were well-mannered children who seldom talked and rarely socialized.

The animals lined both sides of Main Street waiting anxiously as the participants lined up in formation for the parade. The mayor and his family set poised and straight in their big fancy shinny black motor cart, decorated with red and white streamers that reached to the ground. Behind the wheel was Carter Weasel, the family chauffeur.

At approximately noon, the mayor would stand and slowly turn to the four hares that stood directly behind the motor cart with horns in hand. They were dressed in bright orange tights and red, yellow and green stripped jackets with orange buttons. With his hands in the air, the mayor would signal the hares to begin playing the marching song. Slowly turning, the mayor would turn and take his seat behind his wife. Carter Weasel would begin driving slowly down the street proudly with a wide grin.

Following the four marching hares with horns were children dressed in decorative costumes, carrying flags and waving to friends and family who assembled to watch them go past. Immediately behind them were assorted floats from different groups, organizations and merchants lined up filled with animals. The floats were decorated with streamers, ribbons and colored paper.

Loud, jolly cries went up when a family of raccoons ranging from toddler to Grandpa Marshall Raccoon appeared dressed in bright oversized customs. Their faces were painted with bright colors and around their mouths were smiles and frowns painted white. Dressed in an assortment of oversized clothes, large curly wigs on their head and gigantic shoes on their feet they tumbled, balanced and pivoted, laughing, shouting comically as they weaved in and out among the procession and the crowd. The children waited in anticipation, as the older raccoons approached them and amazed them with feats of magic. Coins and other objects were taken from their ears or some other part of their body. One time Grandpa Raccoon walked up to a crying child and out of the blue, a large lollipop appeared! The most experienced clowns were a family of raccoons. A parade was not a parade unless it had a band, and there were two bands. One from the local high school and the second band consisted of seniors. Their uniforms consisted of powder blue jackets and trousers with a wide yellow stripe down the sides, black patent leather boots above the calf and a white felt wide brimmed hats with a blue feather in the brim. The band had practiced for the past four Saturdays and it showed as they predicted played off-tune. No one seemed to notice when they occasionally marched out of step. Behind them were a company of bicyclists and several decorated carriages pulled by chirping robins. Following them was the float carrying the newly elected Queen of Summer. Out of the fifty young girls, competing, only one was chosen each year.

The competition was always held in the castle and during the first year of Saul's reign, Thelma the youngest daughter of Adam Beaver was crowned queen. When her name was called, she first screamed and then she cried as she hugged last year's winner. Her family was so happy that they jumped up and down, shouting with glee.

After some time, Thelma was able to compose herself and accepted the bouquet of flowers that were handed to her. Last year's winner, Tiana Skunk, escorted her up to the king. She was afraid and excited at the same time as she bowed before the king.

The castle was beautiful, more beautiful than she could have ever imagined.

Everything in and outside the castle was painted in white and gold. All the doors were double, tall and painted gold. The white walls were decorated with gold mirrors, sconces and an array of portraits of past kings and their families.

From a distant, she had observed the king sitting on the throne, his gaze wondering lazily over the crown. He looked bored, hoping, knowing, and fulfilling his duty as a king.

Saul was young for a king, she thought straining to see him better. It was very hard as the other contestants were pushing and jostling each other to get a better view.

As Thelma stood before the king, she was trembling so badly that she was afraid she would faint from the excitement. It was a rare privilege just to be in the king's presence. She had heard rumors that the king stood a head taller than all the hares. Standing before him, she realized that it was true. He did stand a head taller than everyone and was very handsome. She tried to remember everything they had practiced over the past two weeks but it was all quickly forgotten.

She curtsied before the king and extended her hand to him. It seemed like an eternity before he grasped her hand and held it to his mouth. He held her hand for the longest as he looked into her eyes. She was so embarrassed that she was afraid she had done something wrong. She had heard wild stories about the king and she now wondered if they were true.

After kissing her hand, he led her to the dance floor. Thelma looked around at her family, friends and those in attendance for guidance, but they were as shocked as Thelma, at the king's action. The mayor, about to speak took several steps but changed his mind and moved backward. Never had the king danced with the winner!

The king, without taking his eyes off Thelma, signaled the orchestra and they began playing a waltz. The king danced with Thelma through two waltzes. The animals did not know what to think of the king's action. After the dance, he walked off the floor and disappeared through a door without saying a word.

No one thought anymore about the king and his strange behavior as they prepared for the yearly festival.

Thelma's father was so proud of this daughter that every time he looked at her, tears of happiness would roll down his face. He even volunteered to design and decorate the float. He labored day and night designing and constructing the float to highlight his daughter's beauty. The float was round and assembled in three tiers. The bottom tier was decorated with large red flowers, the middle tier adorned with red and yellow flowers, entwined with green shrubs. The top tier was garnished with large yellow and white flowers with tiny red flowers settling in the midst of them. Housed in the middle of the float was a gold throne and sitting on the throne with a smile on her face and a large bouquet of flowers in her arm was Thelma, the new queen of summer. She smiled at the crowd, waving and blowing kisses. Her hair was pulled upward on her head and nestled in the front was a beautiful silver tiara with sparking diamonds. She wore a long white gown with prints of small red and yellow roses. Her mother had worked for two months, to make sure the dress was ready in time for the festival event. Beneath the float and riding on motorbikes were her proud father, two brothers and an uncle.

The royal family was always at the end of the parade. In the past years, the royal family would sit on thrones carried by the soldiers and hired workers. After Saul became king, everything changed. The royal family now rode in a single motor cart in front of the soldiers. His mother was not happy with the arrangement as she sat in the cart with her daughters closed lipped neither looking left nor right.

His mother was more upset that they were not allowed to purchase new clothes than have to sit in the open motor cart. Over the months, she and her daughters had lost considerable weight because of their restricted diets. Their clothes were too large, hanging loosely on their bodies. It was embarrassing enough to have on last year's gown but to have them ill-fitting, was devastating. He would not allow their clothes to be altered, stating that they needed to learn to do more things on their own. The nerve of that man! They were the royal family and should be treated like royalty, not like peasants. No matter how hard she pleaded, begged and tried to go behind his back, she could not persuade any of the royal workers to go against her son's orders.

This morning she confronted her son and flatly refused to attend the festivities. Saul threatened her that if they didn't get dress and ready in half-an-hour, he would have the soldiers drag them out to the cart no matter what they had on. She did not believe him until he gave orders to Captain Beaver to have the soldiers to escort his family in half an hour regardless of how they were dressed. They dressed in haste, all the time hating the king, and wishing their father was still alive.

Directly behind the royal family marched the soldiers dressed in their black and green uniforms with spears in hand, led by Captain Beaver. In the midst of the soldiers was the king sitting high on a gold throne. He was neither smiling, nor waving to the crowd.

As the parade passed, the animals fell in behind the procession nervously awaiting the outcome of the day. By the time they reached the clearing, the animals were ready for some fun, games and food.

As the animals poured into the clearing, the adults greeted each other with hugs and kisses. The younger children chased each other around their parents, laughing and playing tag. They were always glad to have a celebration. The teenagers were more modest in their greeting. They would stand by their parents, shyly glancing away all the time with a smile on their face. Since the last celebration many of them had grown up and had become more aware of the opposite sex.

After their greeting, they gathered at their special places and set up their tables with the delicious food they had prepared just for the occasion.

The men would hover to the side, exchanging stories, each one more elaborate than the other. The women remained close to their tables, striving to display their goodies to the best advantage as they kept a weary eye on the younger children. With babies in arms, the mothers chattered among themselves, whispering, laughing and commenting on how the children had grown over the past year.

The young male's, apart from admiring the opposite sex, were waiting for the contests to begin, in order to prove their strength and power in such skills as archery and wrestling. There were prizes for the winners of each contest, all to be awarded with great ceremony by Mayor Samuel Beaver.

As the young men waited for the contests to begin, they did silly things to attract the attention of the opposite sex. They would do cartwheels, play fight, or shove each other, all the time whispering among themselves and never taking their eyes off of their audience. The young girls pretended that they didn't see them, but they did through half-closed eyes. They hovered and whispered among themselves glancing at the young boys' antics. The younger children were oblivious to what was happening. They were in their own world as they mingled freely among the chattering adults, always keeping watchful eyes. When the adults were not looking, they would lurk near or under the table to snatch bits of food. This was a special time for the animals as they had prepared for this event for a whole year.

After everyone had settled down, the animals would gather around the platform. All eyes were on Mayor Samuel Badger as he kept pulling out his vest pocket watch.

When the time was right, the mayor with grace and dignity walked up the steps to the platform followed by his wife and children. After his family was seated, he walked up to the podium to begin his speech. The mayor was a proud Badger and which showed in his long and boring speech about how proud he was to be their mayor and all the wonderful things he had done over the years. The animals had learned to tolerate the exhausting speeches and waited patiently for him to conclude.

When the speech finally ended, they would shout, throw their hats in the air and clap their hands. Now the fun could begin as they moved to an open meadow where the first game would commence.

The three-legged race was the favorite of the animals, especially the fathers. It gave them the opportunity to pair up with their sons to see who was the fastest. Afterward, mothers and daughters paired up and ran the same race. It was fun to see, because the women wore dresses, and would trip over them. It took twice as long for them to run the race than the males.

Saul knew that the animals were apprehensive of him, so he wanted to please them and thought it would be equally fun to have father and daughters, and the mother and sons run the sack race. But the most brilliant idea was to have the parents paired up to run the three-legged races. The children thought it was hilarious to watch their parents struggling to the finish-line with dirt on their faces and sometimes torn clothes.

After the sack races there was archery, horseshoe pitching, and volleyball. While the games were going on, others tried out for the talent contest, bobbing for apples, and other games of skill and chance. There was something for every age including the babies. They called it the *Diaper*

Race. In this contest, the parents tried to get their babies to crawl to them and the event always drew a large crowd.

After everyone had worked up a hearty appetite and the awards had been given, it was time to eat the delicious food that had been prepared. There was so much food to choose from that many were able only to snack. When it seemed that they could not eat another bite, it was time for the pie-eating contest. This was the favorite of all the youngsters. They had the opportunity to eat all the sweets they wanted with their hands and don't have to be nice about it.

This year winner, with cherry all over his face was Thomas Squirrel. He was tinnier and shorter than all the contestants, but he could eat. His father told everyone that his son had a hollow leg and was stuffing the food in it while he ate. To see him eat, one would have believed the tale.

After the games had ended and the food consumed, the musicians gathered their instruments and began strumming a tune. The older and younger adults paired off and began dancing joyfully around the great tree. The animals danced, laughed and clapped their hands and feet to the beat of the music. The children mimicked their parents as they danced on the outskirts of the circle.

In the late afternoon the festival celebration came to an end as the last tune was played. Parents began to disperse as they sought out their families and began the tedious task of packing their belongings and saying goodbye to their friends and loved ones. Some they would not see again until next year.

"Subjects," Saul said standing on the platform. "I know we have all had a wonderful and joyous time."

The crowd cheered and whistled showing their delight.

"But the fun isn't over," he said.

The crowd fell silent. Each one looked at each other in confusion.

"It's not over?" someone questioned.

"What did we forget?" someone else asked.

They were confused by the king's words. They had had the parade, the games and eaten food until they couldn't eat anymore and danced until their feet hurt. What event could they have forgotten?

No one spoke and hoped the king would explain what they had forgotten.

"The day is early and I thought it would be fun to add one more activity."

The animals nodded their agreement. What other activity did their king have in mind, they could not imagine. They hoped it was short and fun like the ones he had incorporated earlier.

The king sensing their hesitation, spoke again a little louder. "I the king challenge the slowest animal to a foot race!" he said stepping down from the platform and with his foot drew a line about five-feet long.

"This year, I challenge the slowest animal in the forest to a foot race," he said proudly as he looked from face to face.

It took a few seconds for the king's words to take root in the animals' minds. Some of the animals took a few steps backward as fear gripped their hearts. The smaller animals were so afraid that they hid behind the bigger and taller ones. They were not about to challenge the king and suffer defeat and humiliation.

"Surely there is one among you?" he asked scanning the crowd. "Please don't be afraid."

Even as the animals murmured among themselves, there was one who was not afraid. Within the quietness and stillness there was a movement from the back of the crowd. A soft voice was heard.

"I accept your challenge, King Saul!"

"What?" the animals mumbled trying to locate where the voice was coming from.

"Who said that?" they asked.

"I accept the king's challenge to a race!" the voice rang out once again.

They looked around wondering who would accept the king's challenge. They saw no one until they lowered their eyes. Slowly and quietly, David the tortoise came forward. When the animals saw who it was, they began to laugh loudly. They knew he was jesting since everyone knew that David was the slowest tortoise around.

As David emerged, the animals formed a semicircle around him trying to get a better view. They laughed and pointed at him. They knew that David was not serious in challenging the king.

David knew that everyone was staring, thinking what a fool he was, but he had accepted the challenge and was not about to back down.

Saul joined in the laughter because he too thought it was ridiculous that

23

David, of all the tortoises, would challenge him. But he did not let the opportunity slip pass when he said, "I accept your challenge, David Tortoise."

Jessie Hare Jr. envisioned David trying to out run the king. It made him laugh so hard that tears formed and his sides hurt. He was laughing so hard that he had to hold his stomach. The animals joined in the laughter as David's challenge was truly comical.

Jessie walked around David and looked at him up and down and once again burst out laughing.

Fighting for control, he spoke. "You challenge the king to a race. Why everyone knows you are the smallest and the slowest tortoise in the forest. A snail could beat you at a race."

The words he spoke were like daggers in David's heart. His eyes filled with tears, but he blinked them back furiously. He was not going to allow anyone to see his hurt.

"Size is not important. It's what's inside that counts," David said standing a little taller with admiration in his voice. He only came up to the waist of Jessie Hare. He was a little afraid but with every bit of strength he possessed, he held his head up.

Daniel Skunk, the youngest of six children, puffed out his chest and stepped forward. "You must have a lot inside if you think you can beat the king," he said joining in the merriment.

"Then why don't you challenge the king?" David asked looking from Jessie Hart to Daniel Skunk. He knew that the animals thought of him as being foolish, but he was not going to let his size keep him from challenging the king.

It became deathly quiet as they stared first at Daniel Skunk and then at Jessie Hare waiting for their reply. Suddenly it was no longer funny.

Daniel Skunk turned, lifted up his head and spoke, "I would have, if you hadn't spoken up first," he said edging toward his mother.

"Daniel," his mother said. "What did you say?"

He looked up at his mother, all innocent with big black marble eyes. "I said, I would have challenged the king, but David beat me to it." He spoke with pride in his voice.

"Daniel," his mother spoke again.

"Yes mother," he said lowering his head.

"I don't want to hear such nonsense coming from your mouth again."

"Yes Mother," he said moving closer his mother. "I'm not afraid of the king," he said barely above a whisper. Stopping next to his mother, he looked up and saw the scorn written on her face and instantly knew he was in trouble.

"Well, I would have if I wasn't so young," he said once again looking down to the ground running his toe in the dirt. He was embarrassed and he felt it was all Jessie Hare's fault.

"But you are not afraid. Are you Jessie?" Daniel Skunk asked looking at Jessie with a smirk on his face.

Feeling cornered, Jessie turned red with embarrassment. Without looking up, he knew everyone was looking at him and he didn't know what to say or do. He looked around and all eyes were upon him waiting for his answer. Beads of sweat surfaced on his forehead as he tried to come up with a reply that would not make him more uncomfortable than he already was. He didn't want them to think he was a coward but he refused to be humiliated by running a foot race against the king. Everyone knew that the king was the tallest, strongest and fastest hare in the land.

"Well, I… that is… I'm too smart to make a fool of myself," he said moving away from David. "Besides, the king said the slowest animal. I can run rings around David," he said escaping into the crowd.

"This is nonsense," Timmy Badger said coming forward. He was dressed in gray overalls and a red handkerchief tied around his neck and one in his back pocket. No matter what the occasion, Timmy Badger always had a red handkerchief around his neck and one in his back pocket.

"David, go home and forget such foolishness. You will only embarrass yourself and your family."

"I see no harm in the king's challenge," David replied.

"You wouldn't," Howard O'Possum said emerging from the crowd and stood near David. "For years, you have always tried to prove yourself and each time you tried, you failed. Now give up this silly idea and go home."

"It's not silly and I don't have to prove anything. The king asked and I volunteered." David would not allow his words to alter his choice; he was too proud and too stubborn. He stood his ground.

"Yes, you volunteered to embarrass yourself and your family. Now forget such nonsense and go home," said Howard O'Possum. "What do you think your mother would say if she could see you embarrassing your family? God rest her soul," he said pulling off his gray felt hat and placing it over his heart. Several others joined him as they to placed their hands over their hearts in respect.

David knew that they would not understand why he challenged the king even if he tried to explain. All they saw was an undersized tortoise. Refusing to listen to their objections, he turned and walked over to the starting line, getting into position. No matter what others said, he was not afraid to challenge the king. He knew he could not win the race, but he believed that against all odds sometimes the impossible happens.

All of David's life had been a struggle and each day he was reminded of his dissimilarity. Even when he was born he had been different from his family. He was sick almost unto death for many months, leaving him smaller and weaker than his sisters and brothers. While all of his family had tan heads and dark brown shells, David had a medium brown head and a light tan shell with dark brown spots. His family stood almost three feet tall while he stood only two feet.

Although he was different, David was a determined tortoise. In the early years he tried to fit in with the others but found it was too painful. Every physical feat he tried, he failed. Those he tried to impress, laughed and teased him. The only thing he was able to compete at successfully with his peers was with his books. Through books, he learned he was as big and tall as anyone.

Even though he rose against his limitation, the animals would not accept him. He learned to never allow words or criticisms of his sizes or color affect how he felt about himself and how he treated others. The words they said about him caused a deep ache deep down inside, but he had learned not to allow it to dictate his attitude toward others.

When David decided it was time to leave home and begin a life of his own he started by searching for a job to support him. He tried to get a job in town using his hands and body, but no one would hire him.

David loved fishing and he decided that he should try to make a living by catching fish. There were several others who tried to make a living at fishing but they were not successful. He could catch several of them a day, but not a large enough amount to support him. Determined to make a living fishing, David spent hours at a time studying them. He observed them swimming back and forth; some swam alone, some in small groups while others swam in large schools. Submerged beneath the water, he swam among them, enjoying himself.

One day David was relaxing in the boat with his eyes closed listening to instrumental music from his portable radio, when he heard noises. Opening his eyes and sitting up, he was amazed to see swarms of fish surrounding his boat. They were drawn to the music. When he turned off the radio, they submerged beneath the water. When he turned it on again, they surfaced swimming near the boat. He couldn't believe his eyes. He was so overjoyed that he rowed around and around the lake laughing and crying at the same time. He had found the secret that he had been searching for. Who would have believed that fish were attracted to music?

Everywhere he went, the fish followed, as long as he played the music. The answer he was searching for was now in his grasp.

After reaching the shore, he danced around before he went to Harry Tortoise to purchase a boat. When Harry learned why David wanted the boat, he laughed and laughed. He went and told others who also thought it was very funny and joined in the laughter. When Harry was able to contain himself, he sold David his boat for half the value because he knew that within several months, he would have it back in his possession. He knew that David of all animals would never make a living catching fish.

David ignored Harry teasing and counted the coins. The price of the boat took all his money but he didn't care as he climbed aboard the boat.

David constructed a net with a microphone attached and on his first day out he brought in such a large catch that it took Gregg Fox and his two sons to help load the fishes in his wagon. News spread quickly of his success. The animals would line the riverbank just to watch David fish. They were baffled by his success. From their viewpoint, they could not see how David was so successful, but every day without fail he pulled in a large catch. Each day there was a different animal that would ask about his fishing technique. He would only smile and continue with his work.

The only one that was not happy about David's success was Harry Tortoise. He was angry because he could have sold the boat to David at twice the price. Because of David's success now, his friends laughed at him.

Now that David was successful at fishing, he was able to buy some land near the river and had a modest cottage built. There he remained until this day.

Even though he was a wealthy merchant, David was still viewed as a short, little tortoise. He had accomplished a lot but the animals' attitude toward him had not changed. Once upon a time their attitude had hurt and shammed him, but that had been a along time ago.

"We'll start here," Saul said pointing at the line he drew with his foot. "Down to Tina Snail's home and back. That's about half a mile," he said smiling.

The animals knew that the race was hopeless for David. A small number of them began to disperse, gathering up their belongings and went home.

"On your mark!" said Captain Beaver with his hand in the air.

"Get set!"

David felt his pulse racing. He was ready.

"Go!" Captain Beaver said dropping his arms.

Saul streaked passed David, almost knocking him off balance.

The animals began to laugh as David slowly ran down the lane hidden in a cloud of dust.

David was only a few yards from the starting line when Saul streaked across the finished line. The animals cheered their king as he pranced around victorious. Saul should have been happy, but he didn't feel like a winner. It was not as much fun as he had first envisioned, especially, when the slow moving tortoise came over the finish-line much later.

Even though David had lost the race, he didn't stop. No, he continued the race. He ran as fast as he could down to Tina Snail's house and back. By that time he returned to the starting line, the animals had packed up their belongings and taken their families' home. He was all alone.

One would have thought he would be sad or disappointed that he did not win. Not David, the important thing was that he tried. He felt proud in challenging the king as he slowly walked home alone. It was only a race and he was destined to lose, but just for a moment he felt important.

The next year for the summer celebration, the day started out as usual –

a bright sunny day with the temperatures in the mid-eighties, but later the perfect day turned into a day the animals would never forget. It was a day etched on the animals' mind for eternity.

The festival started out as usual with the mayor and his family leading the parade. This year winner of the Queen of Summer was Nancy Chipmunk. After the parade, the animals congregated around the big oak tree as usual. Once again this year's winner of the pie-eating contest was Thomas Squirrel.

After the dance, the animals were cleaning up and preparing to return home and were surprised when their king once again took to the podium and challenged the slowest animal to a foot race again. The animals remembered what had happened the previous year. Within minutes the king had defeated David who was only a few yards from the starting line.

Saul felt confident that several would step forward to challenge him. He felt good when he won the race last year, and he knew he would feel even better this year.

When no one stepped forward, Saul once again made the challenge.

"Surely, there must be someone in your midst who is not afraid to challenge the king to a foot race."

He was greeted with silence. No one dared to step forward and be humiliated.

A small voice was heard in the midst of the crowd. The animals look down and there was David coming forward!

Saul was disappointed when David stepped forward. He remembered last year. It was no fun to race against him. He was just too slow.

Ignoring David, Saul spoke again. "Surely, someone feels lucky today," he said as he began to dance around. Still no one else stepped forward. Disappointed, Saul walked down to the starting line. He looked over and saw a bright smile on David's face. This made Saul very angry and he glared at him. He was so angry that he moved away from the starting line. He didn't want to race against David. He was just too slow.

As he moved away, the animals began to murmur among themselves as they watched their king walk away. Stopping only a few yards from his soldiers, he saw surprise and disappointment written on their faces. Turning around and facing the crowd, he realized he had made a grave error. If he walked away from this race, he would never again have the respect of the animals.

"Let the race begin," he said jogging back to the finished line. He tried to smile but it only came out as a grimace.

The animals breathed a sigh of relief, as the king returned to the starting line. A loud cry and clapping was heard by the animals as they cheered their king.

As the signal was given to begin the race, Saul changed his tactic. Instead of speeding ahead, he began harassing David by running circles around him and encouraging him to run faster. The younger crowd enjoyed the king's antics as they too laughed and joined in the merriment, encouraging David to run faster.

Growing tired of the teasing, Saul speeded down the lane down to Tina's Snail house. Looking back, he did not see any sign of David so he walked down to the river and began skipping stones across the water as he envisioned his victory reception. At first he was upset when David stepped forward to accept his challenge, but now he realized that his victory would be glorious. Racing against a tortoise was not fun. There wasn't any reason to expel so much energy against a slow moving animal. After some time he became weary and sleepy and laid down on the soft grass and took a short nap.

After some time had passed and there was no sign of the king or David, the animals began to worry. Instead of going home, they put away their bundles and stood at the starting line, looking for their king to appear. The animals had only a view of a fourth of a mile because the lane veered left and heavy foliage grew near the lane.

Half an hour later, the animals could not believe their eyes. Coming slowly down the road was David and the king was nowhere in sight.

"It's David," shouted one of his brothers.

"David?"

"It couldn't be."

"I can't believe my poor eyes," said Jonathan Raccoon as he peered down the lane. Cleaning his spectacles with a handkerchief he put them back on and once again peered down the lane. "It is David."

It was whispered among them. *"Could it be that the tortoise could possibly win the race? Where was the king? Could something have happened to their king? Could David win the race?"*

All at once the crowd came to life as they realized that David could be the winner. When David left the thicket of the bushes, he saw the finish line-up ahead. The crowd was cheering for him. He was so tired he could hardly move his legs. He kept looking over his shoulder expecting to see the king. He wondered *was he hiding in the trees watching him?* Glancing to his left and right he searched for the king, but he could not see him. David was so short that he couldn't see very much of anything, especially over the tall grass but he tried.

He felt that the king was hiding in the thickets of the trees watching him. He knew that the king wanted to humiliate him and as soon as he get within inches of the finished line he would streak by, winning the race.

When Saul awakened, he stretched and looked at the time. He had slept longer than he anticipated and by now David should be nearing the finished line. He smiled as he visualized his subjects carrying him on his shoulders, shouting his victory as he ran as fast as he could. Coming out of the thickets, the finish line came into view. He saw the crowd cheering David, as he was only inches from the finished line. Saul laughed at their foolishness. His victory would be magnificent.

Breathing hard, David kept running, glancing over his shoulder. From behind, he saw a cloud of dust as the king came racing down the road. So the king had been waiting until he neared the finished line. He was disappointed but he continued toward the finish line.

Victory was within his reach. Only a few more inches and he would be at the finish line. Saul was right behind him. David's hopes were crumbling before his eyes. Once again Saul would win and he would be humiliated.

He could not hear the king behind him because of the roar of the crowd but he could see the cloud of dust in his wake. Fear gripped his heart as his heart thudded so hard in his chest, it hurt. Please Lord, he prayed, please allow me to win this race.

Captain Beaver quickly summoned one of the soldiers and they took several pieces of yellow streamer, braided them and secured them between two chairs across the finished line. He was proud of what he had done and hoped that the king would appreciate his efforts. For a minute he was worried when he saw David coming down the lane and the king was nowhere in sight. But when he saw the king coming out of the thicket, his heart jumped with glee. It was just like the king to make a triumphant entry.

The race was close as Saul streaked across the finished line. As the dust settled, everyone was quiet as they looked from their king to David.

Saul danced around basking in his victory. He went up to David and shook his hand.

"It was a good race and I'm sorry you didn't win."

David shook his hand and accepted defeat. He tried his best and that was what was most important.

The animals came up and congratulated the king and shook his hand, totally ignoring David. Some were a little disappointed that David did not win. For the first time, they saw David in a different light. It took courage and determination to challenge the king.

"You had us worried there for a while Your Majesty, but in the end you came through," Captain Beaver said shaking the king's hand with a big grim on his face.

"Let's hear it for the king!" the captain shouted. The soldiers hoisted him up on their shoulders as they danced around and around praising the king.

Hurrah for the king! Hurrah!
Hurrah for the king! Hurrah!
The king is the winner! Hurrah!

Saul signaled the animals to put him down.

"Everyone please quiet down!" Saul shouted, getting the crowd's attention.

"Today we had a wonderful time. We had a glorious parade, good food and a race of speed. We should all congratulate David on his efforts even though he lost the race."

Saul was happy as he looked at his subjects. He was so happy that he began to jump around trying to calm his racing feeling.

Earl Squirrel stepped forward and spoke. "I uh … that is, I mean … David didn't loose the race. Oh, dear… he's the winner!"

"David, the winner," the animals began to mumble among themselves. How could this be possible?

"What?" the king shouted. Saul knew he had not heard Earl Squirrel correctly. He was the winner not that slow moving tortoise!

In a squeaky voice Earl spoke up. "David is the winner."

"That's impossible. I was across the line before him."

"Uh… You see… That's not true King Saul," nervously Herman Skunk said as he walked forward with a picture in his hand. Herman Skunk was the owner and editor of the local newspaper. He took pictures of each event and of every winner. Sometimes it was his photos which helped decide who was the winner.

Today was the first time in history Herman Skunk wished he had forgotten his camera. When he took the picture out of the camera and realized that David was the winner and not the king, he was surprised and was trying to decide what to do with the picture when Earl Squirrel walked up behind him.

"I can't believe my eyes," he said directly behind Herman Skunk.

Before Herman could speak up, Earl Squirrel spoke those dreadful words. "David is the winner."

Herman Skunk looked at Earl Squirrel with contempt in his eyes.

Now everyone knew that David was the winner and he had no choice but to speak up. He had a very bad feeling that David being the winner would not set too well with the king.

He stood before the king with the evidence in his hand. He tried to speak but the lump that formed in his throat prevented him. With a finger, he ran it around the starched white shirt collar. He must speak with his wife about not having the laundry put so much starch in his shirts.

"See," he said. His hand was trembling so badly that he was unable to steady the picture. "David was under the finish line before you."

Saul snatched the picture from Herman Skunk's hand and glared at the picture. It was true David's head was under the finish line before he reached the ribbon.

" David is the winner," voices began to mumble as they peered over Saul's shoulder looking at the picture.

"David is the winner!" Earl Squirrel said proudly in a loud voice.

"Hurrah!" David's brother shouted looking at the picture. "I can't believe it. David you won!"

33

The animals rushed toward David, hoisting him up on their shoulders.

David was too stunned to stop the animals from picking him up and settling him on their shoulders. The animals were so excited that they began to march around with him on their shoulder singing:

"Hurrah! Hurrah! Hurrah!
David is the winner!
David is the winner!
Hurrah! Hurrah!
He has defeated the king!
Hurrah! Hurrah!
David! David!
Hurrah! Hurrah! Hurrah!"*

Over and over they shouted. This was a wonderful time for the animals. Never in history had anything as exciting and wonderful ever happened. This was a time for rejoicing and celebration, as they carried David on their shoulders.

David closed his eyes and then opened them again as he scanned the crowd and saw many happy faces. They were actually cheering him and praising him. A wide smile spread across his face as tears of happiness surfaced and rolled down his tiny cheeks. He had won the race and Herman Skunk had the picture to prove it. David, the slowest tortoise in the forest had actually beaten Saul the faster hare in the land across the finished line. He was happy because he had done the impossible. No more would they call him, *David the slow moving tortoise, but **David who had defeated the fastest hare in the land**.*

With the picture in his hand, the king had to admit that David's head was under the finished line before him.

Herman Skunk reached for the picture in Saul's hand, but he held fast to the picture. Panic filled him as an alarm sounded in Herman's head as he drew back and looked at the king's face. He knew that the picture would not make the king happy but the look on the king's face was that of scorn. It's quite embarrassing to learn that the slowest animal in the forest actually beat the fastest hare. Now the look the king gave him scared him down to his toes. The panic turned into a knot in his stomach, knotting into a hard ball. He began to back away until he was at a safe distance. He hastily gathered up his equipment and searched the crowd for his wife and son. Finding his wife, he grabbed her hand and bade her to get their son and leave quickly.

"Missy," a nickname he calls his wife. "Find our son and follow me home quickly,"

She started to speak, but when she saw the fear and panic in his eyes, she knew from experience that something was wrong. Something had frightened her husband and when something frightened Herman, it had to be for a good reason. Once they were home and behind closed doors, she knew her husband would explain his hasty retreat.

Searching for her son, she saw that he was talking to Cindy Skunk who was a couple of years younger than he. She was a nice girl but her family was poor. She had hoped her son would be attracted to Rita Skunk, whose family owned a radio station in the next kingdom. Rita wasn't as pretty as Candy but she was a nice girl. She grabbed her son's hand and began pulling on him, urging him to follow her.

"Johnny, come quickly. Come quickly," she continued to utter as she pulled on his arm. He didn't want to leave but when he saw the fright in her eyes he decided that he should follow her.

Candy grabbed his arm. "Wait Johnny! What's wrong?" she asked running to keep up. "Why are you leaving?"

"I don't know but I must follow my mother." Johnny slowed his steps to a saunter causing his mother to slow down.

"Why?"

Glancing from his mother to Candy, he felt pulled in two directions. His mother's vice-like grip caused a sliver of fear to run down his spine. Her face was pale, her hands trembling and sweaty as her eyes darted back and froth. He looked around but could not see any immediate danger. *If there was danger he should warn Candy and her family.*

"Mother, what's wrong? Why do I have to leave now?" The more he tried to talk to his mother the more nervous she became as tears surfaced and rolled down her eye. Now he was frightened and he didn't know why.

"Candy, I'll come over tomorrow and talk to you, but right now I have to go with my mother," he said walking away.

He quickly gathered up their belongings and followed her. When he spotted his father, he seemed nervous and frightened as he kept looking toward the crowd. As they left the gathering, his father was almost running.

None of the animals witnessed the Skunks' speedy departure, they were having too much fun. It was not every day something like this happened.

While the animals danced around rejoicing in David's glorious victory, the king stood glaring at them. Only a few moments ago they were cheering and rejoicing for him and now the tortoise was in the spot light. The more the king looked at the merriment before him, the angrier he became. He was so angry that he saw orange and then bright red. He stood rigid and tense, his eyes stone-cold with his hands on his hips. His cheeks were puffed out, his eyes huge and glaring at the animals.

He scanned the crowd for James Beaver, the captain of the soldiers. When he spotted him, his anger increased two-fold. The captain was sworn to protect the king with his life and there he was on the edge of the crowd dancing, laughing and having a good time. *How dare he cheer for that slow moving tortoise!* Saul was so enraged that he wanted to punch someone, but there was no one around to take his frustration out on. If it wasn't for that ribbon and the picture, he would have been declared the winner.

Saul signaled to one of the soldiers that stood nearby enjoying the merriment. When he glanced at the king and saw the scorn on his face, his heart skipped a beat. The king did not look happy, in fact he looked downright furious. The merriment he was feeling faded as the color drained from his face.

When he saw the king signal him, he felt trapped. He looked around and wondered what best route to take. There was no place to escape. It took all his strength to make his legs obey as he walked over to the king.

"Soldier, what do you see that was amusing?"

"Nothing sir," the soldier said trembling. He didn't know what he had done to make the king angry, but he wished he were somewhere else at that moment

"Then why were you smiling?" the king demanded.

Raymond Squirrel looked at the king with astonishment written all over his face. He didn't know how to respond to the king's question.

"Soldier did you hear me!" the king demanded.

"I don't know why, sir." Raymond Squirrel could feel the sweat rolling off his face. He felt he was being punished for something he didn't know anything about.

Saul just glared at him. Finally he spoke, "Get Captain Beaver," he said through clenched teeth.

Raymond turned and nearly fell over his own feet in his haste to leave. He shoved his way through the crowd trying to reach the captain.

"Captain," he said coming up behind him and tapping him on the shoulder.

The captain ignored him as he continued dancing with his daughter.

"Captain," Raymond said louder and once again tapping the captain on the shoulder. "The king wants to see you and he doesn't seem very happy."

"Why are you disturbing me?" the captain said turning to look at Raymond. "Now leave me alone," he said through clenched teeth.

"I said, the king wants to see you and he's angry about something."

"Not as angry as I am at you right now."

The captain closed his eyes as he fought for control. He didn't believe the soldier, but to get him to leave him alone, he spanned the crowd but he didn't see the king.

He was about to resume his merriment until Raymond pointed toward the king. Suddenly the captain stopped dead in his tracks, as his eyes fell on the king.

"Good God man why didn't you tell me?" the captain said as the smile faded, replaced with dread. The king was so angry one could almost see smoke coming out of his ears.

"I tried to tell you captain," Raymond said above a whisper. "I wonder what made him angry?"

"The only way we'll find out is to ask him," he said rushing to the king's side.

"Sir?" Captain Beaver asked coming up to the king with confusion written on his face.

"I want this crowd dispersed immediately," he said with his brown eyes blazing.

"Immediately, sir?"

"By force if necessary."

"By force?" he asked looking around. "Why sir? Has something happened?"

Saul ignored his questions as he glared at him. "Captain, are you hard of hearing?"

The captain swallowed nervously and licked his dry lips.

"No … sir," he said stammering.

"Immediately!" the king ordered sharply.

Captain Beaver was about to speak and realized his error. He turned and ordered Raymond Squirrel to summons the soldier.

The soldiers assembled with confused looks on their faces.

"Hey Captain!" Charles Rabbit called out. "Why did you call us away from the celebration?"

"Yes, we were having fun. It's not everyday David wins a foot race," Walter Rabbit said, smiling. He especially liked the merriment. He liked David and was happy that he had won the race.

Captain Beaver was so angry by their comments that he walked up to Walter Rabbit, standing face to face, staring him in the eyes. Through clenched teeth, he spoke. "I am not going to say this but once. Never ever question me again. When I call you to order, you are to remain quiet until I speak! Do you understand?"

"Hey captain, there's no reason for you to jump down Walter's throat. He was just asking a question," Donald Brown Beaver said laughing.

"This is not a laughing matter, so get that smile off your face soldier!" he said looking at Donald Brown Beaver who continued to smile.

"The king has ordered that this crowd be disbursed immediately, with force if necessary."

The smiles left the soldier's face.

"Force? Captain you're not serious?" Donald Brown Rabbit said walking over to the captain.

Before Captain Beaver could reply, the king walked up. He had heard the conversation and was not happy the way things were going. Over the years the soldiers had become complacent; soft like their captain. It was up to him to turn them around and be soldiers.

"Is there a problem Captain in carrying out my orders? Or should I appoint someone else who knows how to follow orders?"

"No sir. I think the soldiers are a little confused."

"I didn't ask the soldiers to think but to carry out my orders!" Saul said through clenched teeth.

"Yes sir," Captain Beaver said as he looked from one soldier to the next.

"Soldiers, you are to take up arms and dismiss this crowd immediately; use force if necessary. If there are any questions or complaints, that soldier will be thrown into jail for a month. Do I make myself clear!"

The soldiers nodded their head in agreement.

"To arms and disperse the crowd immediately!"

The soldiers quickly gathered up their spears without a word spoken. They were as confused as the captain. The animals were their friends and families and now they were to disperse them by force if necessary.

Pushing his way through the crowd, the captain stood on the platform.

"Everyone, please be quiet!" he shouted. "I said be quiet!"

Only a few of the animals turned to see what the captain was screaming about.

"By the order of the king. You are to disperse and leave quickly."

"What's the meaning of this Captain Beaver?" Mayor Beaver said walking up to the podium. He was disturbed by the captain's order. He had no right.

"Why are you ordering us to disperse? You have no right," he said as he peered up at the captain.

Suddenly the laughter and merriment ceased as all eyes were focused on the captain.

"Yes, why are you acting cocky all of a sudden, Captain?" Harry Tortoise asked coming up behind the mayor.

"Who put a burr in your underwear?" a voice rang out among the crowd. The animals began laughing as they turned away from him.

The captain was about to answer but the scorn written on the king's face told him enough time had passed.

"Soldiers, dismiss this crowd by force!"

The eyes of the soldiers grew wide with fear.

The crowd stood with their mouths agape as they watched the soldiers encircling them with swords pointed. Panic began to sit in but they didn't know what course of action to take. Some thought it was a game and began to laugh. A few didn't see it as funny and fled down the road. The animals watched and began chuckling at the fleeing animals.

Harry Tortoise was watching the departing animals when he felt something sharp in his ribs.

"Ouch!" he screamed aloud with pain. Looking down he saw red liquid oozing from where the pain was. Looking at the tip of the spear he saw something red on the tip. He once again looked down at the red liquid that had stained his brown vest. Suddenly it hit him like a ton of brick. The soldier had actually wounded him. His eyes grew large as his mouth opened and suddenly everything turned black as his body slumped to the ground.

Those around him saw what had happened and panicked. In their haste to flee, they knocked the soldier down to the ground that had injured Harry Tortoise stepping on him. Had he not contracted his body into a ball and rolled away from the crowd he would have been killed.

Screams of pain echoed through the crowd as the swords pierced several others. Suddenly the crowd went wild as panic raced through them like a wild fire in the middle of summer. In their haste to escape many were knocked to the ground and trampled. Spears were knocked from the soldiers' hands and several were knocked to the ground and stepped on. Acting quickly, they kept rolling until they were out of harms way. The soldiers who were knocked to the ground were angry as they gained their feet and found their spears, looking for revenge.

Tables and chairs were overturned as animals stumbled over them. Those that were injured did not linger as they gained their feet and limped home as quickly as possible.

Trying to stay out of harm's way, the ones who had David on their shoulders, slowly and not so carefully dropped him to the ground and moved almost as one backward.

Sensing his body falling, David retreated into his shell before his body hit the hard ground and rolled several yards.

The confusion was so chaotic that families were separated. Women were screaming for their children. Children were crying as they searched for their parents. Some of the soldiers were more forceful than others, as they drew blood from the panicked crowd.

Saul stood near the platform and watched the animals panic, running into each other as they fled from the soldiers. Such a sight should have given him comfort but it didn't. He was still angry. When some of the soldiers began pushing, shoving and even drawing blood from the animals, he did not intervene nor did he allow the captain to correct the soldiers.

When David's body came to rest, he peered out from his shell watching the confusion. Standing upright, he tried to see what was going on. He heard what the captain had said, but he could not understand why he had ordered the soldiers to disburse the crowd by force. He tried to see what was going on but there were too many fleeing animals surrounding him, blocking his view. Trying to get a better view, he stood on tiptoes but still couldn't see much more than an array of legs, waists and shoulders as they ran in fear. He was afraid and drew back a step and bumped into someone. Before he could utter a word of apology, the animal had vanished. The urge to retreat back into the safety of his shell was overwhelming, but he needed to see what was going on.

In all the chaos, Thelma Beaver was looking for her parents. Mayor Badger hurried across the clearing, hugging tightly to his wife's favorite punch bowl tightly to his chest, and collided with Thelma. As Thelma plummeted downward, the mayor threw his arms up to catch her fall. Instead, the container he was carrying, filled with red punch, went up in the air and splashed all over her. Her forehead caught his nose, throwing him off balance knocking him to the ground. Thelma landed on her backside in the spilled punch. She groaned as a wave of dizziness swept over her. Her head throbbed. She closed her eyes and waited for the dizziness to pass. Her body went very still as she felt liquid oozing down her back and chest. Opening her eyes, she saw the red punch all over her favorite blue dress. She looked at her predicament and taking the only course possible, she began to wail.

The mayor quickly recovered and was about to apologize as he rose to his feet. He halted with the sound of his pants ripping.

He turned red with embarrassment. From his inspection, he realized that the rip was large and in the middle of his backside. He hoped that the rip could be repaired, because these were his favorite pants. Thank God he had on clean underwear. His wife was always reminding him to put on clean underwear.

"Oh, dear, dear, dear," he said. "Oh my!" he repeated as he tried to cover the rip with his hands. He looked around to see if anyone saw his predicament. No one noticed as they fled from the soldiers.

"This is not good. My wife is not going to be happy," he said eyeing the bowl lying in the dirt.

"Oh my and her good punch bowl lying in the dirt," he said reaching to pick up the bowl. Once again the sound of ripping was heard.

"These are my good pants. What will my wife say?" he said straightening.

Thelma's cries penetrated his confused mind. He looked at her and immediately he felt embarrassed. There she sat in the mud with her blue print dress splattered with punch.

"My dear, I'm sorry. Let me help you up," he said reaching with his right hand. "With all the confusion going on, I forgot my manners."

While the mayor was helping Thelma up, a soldier came up behind him. When he saw the mayor bending over revealing the rip in his pants and the red underwear, he couldn't help himself as he pointed his spear where the pants were ripped.

"Ohhhh!" the mayor screamed as he straightened up and grasped his backside with one hand. When the mayor straightened, he released Thelma's hand and she plummeted to the ground, sitting in the spilled punch that was now mixed with the dirt.

"Red underwear? Getting kind of kinky there, mayor," the soldier said laughing.

"Oh my." Ripping his pants was bad enough but to reveal to the world his red underwear was another thing. Once his wife had seen them in a catalog and decided to order a dozen of them because he loved red. He never thought the world would learn his secret.

"Get moving," the soldier said laughing as he once again stabbed the mayor in his backside. The mayor turned around and eyed the soldier, then the spear that was pointed at him. Eyes wide with fear, he threw up his hand releasing the punch bowl and ran screaming down the road. The bowl went up in the air and landed on the soldier's foot, causing him to cry out in pain. Angrily, he limped over to an overturned chair. Righting it, he sat down rubbing his injured toes and saying words that were not used in mixed company.

As Thelma sat in the mud crying, Earl Squirrel was running away from one of the soldiers when he tripped over her, landed face down in the mud beside her.

"Why are you sitting in my way?" he asked with his face and hands covered with mud and dirt.

Momentarily distracted by Earl, Thelma had stopped crying. For a moment she just stared at him. Suddenly and without warning, she let out a wail.

Gaining his feet, Earl Squirrel wiped his hands on his shirt mumbling. Pulling his shirt from his pants, he wiped the dirt from his face.

"Girls!" Earl exclaimed shaking his head. Without another word he disappeared into the thick foliage.

Thelma's father saw her dilemma and hastily came to her rescue. He assisted her to her feet and tried to remove as much dirt and mud from her dress as possible. He pulled out a handkerchief and tried to wipe as much soil from her face as possible.

"Papa, my dress, it's ruined!" she exclaimed.

"There will be others," he said taking her hand. He smiled. He was doing his best to make a bad situation better.

The soldier who had accosted the mayor came up behind Adam Beaver.

"Away with you," he said point his spear with a smile on his face.

Adam Beaver turned and glared at the soldier who spoke. It was Travis Otter who was a friend of his son.

Adam Beaver could not understand what had happened today. Friends were suddenly enemies, all because of a childish foot race. In all the confusion, animals were bumping into each other in their haste to leave. Food was strewn all over the ground, children were crying because they had gotten separated from their parents, and the soldiers were pushing and shoving anyone who was in their way. Some of the animals had sustained injury and wounds from the soldiers.

Adam Beaver forced himself to remain calm. He wanted to flee with the others, but his daughter's well being came first. He glared at the soldier.

"Hurry along," Travis Otter, said barely above a whisper.

Refusing to be rushed, Adam Beaver turned his attention back to his

43

daughter.

"We have more to worry about than a ruined dress my dear," he said taking his daughter's hand and walking at a fast pace toward home.

Soon the clearing was deserted of animals as they dispersed to their homes, locking their doors. For the first time since Saul had taken the throne the animals feared for their lives. Never had they seen their king so angry and upset.

The only animals that were left were Saul, the soldiers and David. The king's face was a mask, twisted in anguish. His fists hung at his sides as he looked around assessing the disaster. Tables were upturned; pots and pans with food in them lay scattered over the ground. Decorations was torn and in a disarray. The once magnificent floats stood deserted along with the band equipment.

Captain James Beaver stood before the king straight and proud. He didn't know what to do or say. He hoped the king was satisfied with the soldiers' display of force. He wasn't and instead felt nausea.

It was some time before the king relaxed and motioned for the captain to bring his throne.

After the animals had retreated, David was able to survey his surrounding and he was greatly surprised. He had heard the harsh command of the captain, shouting of the soldiers and the crying of the children. Never in the history of the kingdom had such disorder and uproar been witnessed.

Even though the animals had fled in panic, David was happy as he began walking home happier than he had been in all of his life. There was nothing he could compare his feeling to because they were so new.

As the soldiers trotted past with the king sitting on the throne with his legs crossed, one of them pushed David aside knocking him off balance. He landed in a ditch, upside down. The soldiers laughed as they continued on their march to the castle. To see David upside down in the dirt with his legs beating the air caused a smile to appear on Saul's face for the first time since he learned David was the winner.

It took David ten minutes just to right himself. He wasn't angry. Today, no this whole year was his and that was something no one could take away from him. As he walked, he would stop along the roadside and smell the flowers and admire the colors before he ate them. Their tastes were sweet and tangy. He especially liked the yellow ones, they were his favorites. They were tangy and filled with ants giving them a unique satisfying taste.

The sun had sunk below the horizon before David reached his home. Opening the backdoor to his cottage, he placed a kettle of water on the stove for his tea. Walking to the cabinets, he took out a cup and saucer for his tea and a blue plate for his cookies. Opening the lid of cookie jar, David smiled. The cookie jar brought back found memories.

It was several years ago. He was feeling a little sad because it was his birthday and no one remembered or wished him well when the doorbell rang. His heart perked up. He had hoped that his family was on the other side of the door. When he opened the door, he was surprised to see Randy Skunk with a package in his hand that was almost as big as him. The box was covered with silver paper and wrapped around the box were red ribbons and a large silver bow on top. Handing him the package, Randy turned and ran away without saying a word.

Taking the box to the kitchen table, he opened it and was surprised to see a white object shaped like a water pitcher and on the top was a small green frog sitting on a lily pad. Opening the lid the odor of ginger floated from the jar. The jar was filled with his favorite cookies; gingersnaps. Since that time, whenever Mrs. Skunk made cookies, she would always send him over a bag.

Taking a cookie out of the jar, he took a bite and savored the flavor as he closed his eyes. *Today*, he thought, *was a day to celebrate* as he took out six more and placed them neatly on a blue plate and carried them to the living room. Setting the plate on the table near his favorite chair, he returned to the kitchen for his tea.

Opening the refrigerator, he took out a small fish and cut it into small pieces and mixed it in with salad greens. With his arms full, he returned to the living room and placed the items on the table next to the cookies. Turning on the stereo, he waited until the music sounded before he settled down into his favorite chair. There was no one there to help him celebrate his victory, but he didn't mind. He had grown accustomed to being alone. He decided that he didn't need a room full of people to feel happy. He didn't think about the king and his reaction for not winning the foot race. No, David thought about the emotions he was feeling as being the winner. His mother had told him not to dwell on his size but on his accomplishments and today he had accomplished something that was once impossible.

While David sat in his comfortable chair listening to soft soothing music, his family and friends afraid, hid from view in their homes. They were groping with the king's reaction for losing the foot race and what kind of retaliation he would inflict upon them because of his loss. It was not their fault that the king had lost the foot race but they knew that everyone would suffer regardless.

The animals had a right to cringe behind closed doors. The very next morning soldiers went throughout the land knocking on doors summoning each family to a meeting at ten outside of the Town Hall.

When the animals arrived in town, Captain Beaver was standing on the podium with a grim look on his face. He had dark shadows under his eyes as if he hadn't slept all night. He was holding tightly in his hand several pieces of paper. Standing behind him fully armed with spears, swords and shields were the soldiers. The animals cringed because they knew that what Captain Beaver had to say was not going to be pleasant.

The sound of iron against iron carried into the streets as the animals gathered at Town Hall. Billowing smoke rose from the blacksmith's chimney. This was quite unusual for a Sunday morning. Melvin Tomcat never worked on Sundays. In less than twenty-four hours so many things had happened. The king lost the foot race with a tortoise, the soldiers using force to disperse the crowd and now they stood fully armed, not only with spears but also swords and shields. They were prepared for battle.

They murmured among themselves. Had war been declared? If so, what town had taken up arms against them and why? The land had been at peace for years. Why had war been declared? They had soldiers, but they were like ornaments for the king.

Talking among themselves they wondered if their new king had made the surrounding towns angry. He didn't have parties like his father and seldom attended parties in the neighboring town. His aloofness could possible cost them their lives.

With compassion the captain's gaze scanned the crowd before him. They were staring at him. Their faces anxiously waited for him to give an account as to why they had gathered. The captain cleared his throat. The animals ceased their talking and focused their attention on him.

"Subjects, our honored king has imposed several new laws that will go into effect immediately," Captain Beaver said wiping the sweat from his brows. His hands were shaking.

The crowd erupted into curious whispers as they awaited the captain to continue.

He was afraid and had been ever since the king had summoned him yesterday. After they had taken the king back to the palace, he immediately summoned the cabinet. For hours they sat listening to the king as he proposed new laws. Laws that would rip the kingdom apart. The cabinet felt it was unfair but the king was beyond listening. No one slept that night, not even the soldiers.

Now he stood before his family, friends and neighbors to announce new laws, laws that would destroy some families. All of his life he had lived here and everyone was his family. He wondered how many were still his friends after his cruel order yesterday. After today, even his family might hate him for doing his duty. For twenty years he had been captain and never had they taken up arms. Never in the history had the soldiers used force upon the citizens. There was no need to delay what he had to read, It must be read as soon as possible.

"Number one – I will read off the names of men who have been drafted into the army as of today. They are to report to the castle at six this evening."

The crowd began to mumble as parents pulled their children closer to them, trying to find solace in the madness.

As the names were called, families cried out in anguish as they hugged their sons. They knew war had been declared and their sons would be killed.

When the captain had finished, a total of one hundred and fifty young men had been inducted into the army. Two of the names called were the captain's youngest sons.

"Why is the king building up the army? Has war been declared?" the animals cried out.

"Yes, why is the king doing this? We already have twenty soldiers, why do we need more?"

The animals were outraged about the sudden increase in the number of their sons drafted into the army without a reason. The next question they asked among themselves, was where the money would come from to pay for the additional soldiers?

Captain Beaver knew they demanded answers but he was given strict orders from the king not to answer one question. He too wanted to know why they were building up the army. The land had been peaceful for years. This was ridiculous to him.

"Number two," the captain said ignoring the questions from the crowd. "Your taxes have increased from five percent to ten percent."

They looked from one to the other, disbelieving what they heard. The animals were insulted.

"Ten percent! Is this a joke, Captain?" someone called out.

"Why is the king doing this!" The cry was heard throughout the citizens.

"Everyone please be quiet!" the captain shouted but the crowd was not paying any attention. The animals were become riled as angry voices were heard and raised fists beat the air. Captain Beaver never dealt with a mob so he didn't know their mentality. But one thing he knew was that they had a life of their own if left unchecked. In a minute the animals would riot and he would be the first they would attack. He must do something quick.

"Soldiers to arms!" the captain, shouted.

The soldiers advanced on the animals ready to attack and even wound the crowd if they continued to advance. They were under orders to kill if needed to keep the animals in check. They were trapped and there wasn't anything they could do.

Slowly, the animals quieted, as all faces turned toward the soldiers.

"If this crowd gets out of order, the soldiers have been ordered to maintain order by any means necessary!" he shouted. "Even to the point of death!"

The crowd halted in their steps. They didn't want a repeat of yesterday. They knew yesterday that the soldiers would do bodily harm if they got out of order.

Eyeing the soldiers, they continued to murmur. They were their husbands and sons and now they had been ordered to use harm if necessary against them once again. Some of the mothers began to cry softly as they watched their sons stand fully armed ready to carry out the captain's order.

Once the crowd had settled down, the captain continued.

"The taxes will be collected at the beginning of each month. Those who are unable to pay their taxes, will be jailed!"

"Jailed?" they cried in one voice.

"We have no jail," someone cried out laughing.

"I'm not going to pay. You can tell the king that," said Calvin Weasel.

"I'm not going to pay either," cried Harry Tortoise.

"You have taken our sons and now you want our money. We won't pay!" cried Calvin Weasel. One by one the words took hold and they animals shouted with fists in the air:

We won't pay.
We won't pay!
We won't pay!
We won't pay!

The captain was in agreement with them but he knew that if they refused to pay, they all would be arrested. Just the thought of having to arrest his friends made the lump in his throat grow larger.

Calvin Weasel looked with admiration on his face. He knew that if the crowd refused to pay, the king was helpless in collecting the taxes.

Suddenly a voice was heard. Gregg Beaver, the brother of captain Beaver spoke up. "Quiet! Quiet!"he shouted. The crowd calmed down and waited to see what the captain's brother had to say.

Gregg Beaver was the younger of the two brothers, the owner of the lumberyard who did all the construction in the kingdom.

"You will pay or go to jail," he said his eyes never leaving his brother's face.

"No! No!" the cries ranged through the crowd.

"Quiet! Let me finish!"

When the crowd quieted, he continued.

"Just this morning I was awakened from my bed by one of the soldiers, the same as you. In his hand was a piece of paper signed by the king. I have been requisitioned to provide a large quantity of lumber, bricks and other building equipment. After hearing my brother speak this morning, I now understand why the order was so huge. It's material for the new jail."

The animals started murmuring again. Gregg Beaver held up his hands, motioning for them to be quiet. "After this meeting, I am to meet with the king about the blueprint of the buildings he wants constructed. I know without a doubt it's the new jail."

"It could be for housing and not a jail," Calvin Weasel said standing near Gregg Beaver.

"With iron bars?"

Calvin was so stunned that he stepped back. He knew without a doubt that the king would jail them if they refused to pay the taxes.

"With the amount of material ordered, the building to be constructed will be large. To my estimation it will accommodate at least a hundred animals at one time."

A cry of anguish like a rolling stone rumbled through the crowd.

Gregg Beaver continued. "The king has anticipated your refusal to pay." Turning, he faced the crowd. "If you refuse to pay, your sons will arrest you and put you in jail. Men how will your family survive while you are locked up?" he asked, challenging the crowd.

They hung their heads in defeat. Gregg Beaver was correct. What could they do? The king would take away their sons and if they didn't pay the taxes, their families would starve and their land seized.

"You can talk. You will be rich off the money the king pays you. Hard earned money from our pockets," John Rabbit cried out in anger.

Gregg Beaver looked at him with animosity in his eyes. "I will lose two sons, two nephews and three cousins to the army. How many sons will you lose John Rabbit?" he asked. John lowered his head. He had four daughters and a son that was in diapers. He was one of the fortunate few with families that were not affected by the king's new army.

"Number three," the captain said, drawing the their attention back to him. "Anyone who wishes to have a party must submit a request to the king's secretary. A fifty-dollar petition fee will be required. Anyone who has a party without a permit will be fined one hundred dollars and all of their property seized. For all children parties, a fee of forty dollars will be required and the party size cannot be no more than five children."

David stood on the outskirts of the crowd and hung his head in sadness as the captain continued to read the new laws. There wasn't anything he could do about it. He knew the animals would blame him, so he turned and slowly walked back home. There wasn't anything he could do but wait to read the king's new laws in the newspaper.

"Number four – Anyone who wishes to speak with the king, must make an appointment with his secretary. A ten dollar fee will be required," the captain said rolling up the paper and handed it to the Herman Skunk to post in the newspaper.

"That is all. Everyone go home and say good-bye to your sons," the captain said stepping down from the podium. Suddenly he felt old, even his steps were slow.

Yes, this was the beginning of a sad kingdom. Over the next several months the half-constructed jail began to fill up as some of the animals refused or could not pay the increased taxes. Sadness, defeat and misery now replaced the laughter and gayety that had once filled the town.

The following year things did not improve for King Saul or the animals. A month before the celebration, the king learned that the animals had gathered and decided to cancel the event. Not to be undermined, the king sent out a decree that anyone that did not participate would be jailed.

The day of the great celebration found the animals apprehensive. All day they could not relax. When the dance was over the animals stood still and silent waiting to see what the king would do.

The king ran up the steps of the platform to the podium with a smile on his face.

Duncan Turtle took a deep, steady breath, clenching his hand until his knuckles hurt. It had taken every ounce of his strength just to get this far. Before the king could make an announcement, he stepped forward.

"King Saul…" the words came out in a squeak. Clearing his throat, Duncan tried again. "King Saul, I volunteer to run the foot race against you."

Duncan was embarrassed and when the king stared at him as if he'd suddenly grown two heads, he thought he would faint. He didn't want to challenge the king, but the money the animals offered him and his family, he could not refuse. They wanted him to challenge the king to a foot race and deliberately loose the race. That was not a problem for Duncan, because he knew he could not outrun the king. He along with the other animals couldn't understand why the king lost the race against David. If it weren't for the pictures Herman Skunk took, none of this would have happened, voicing the sentiment of others. Ever since the king lost the foot race, this cry had ringed throughout the land.

He stood rooted to a spot at the edge of the crowd, waiting. A small wave of relief had rippled through him when Saul had finally taken to the platform. Now he stood before the king, challenging him to a foot race. He tried to smile but the expression on the king's face made him cringe with fear. The king's eyes narrowed into hard slits with an expression that caused Duncan to take several steps backward. He was nervous. His face was perspiring. Beads of sweat rolled off his forehead near his eyes. He could wipe the sweat away from his face but he couldn't wipe the sweat that had gathered under his armpits and alone his spine. He drew a rumpled dirty handkerchief from his pocket and wiped his sweaty forehead. He wished it wasn't so hot. It felt as if it was a hundred degrees in the shade and climbing.

Everyone could see that he was terrified. One could almost smell the fear on him. Duncan kept wiping the sweat from his forehead. Seconds seemed like minutes to him as fear settled in his stomach and he felt like fleeing. If he did that, he would have to give the money back to the merchants. His family needed the money desperately.

The look of panic in Duncan's eyes made the king feel sorry for him but his anger caused him to ignore his request. Averting his eyes and ignoring Duncan, Saul spoke. "Subjects, I your king challenge David Tortoise to a foot race."

After the king made the announcement, Duncan could feel the knot in his stomach slowly begin to untangle. He had challenged the king and he had refused. He had lived up to his part of the bargain.

Sharon Skunk's hold on her husband's arm was like a vice grip and when the king made the announcement, her husband felt her grip slackens. Turning, he was about to speak, when he noticed that she had fainted. He was so nervous he couldn't do anything but hold her hand.

Dr. Woody Raccoon pushed his way through the crowd to the fallen woman. He made a quick examination and as assigned one of the men to carry Mrs. Skunk to his cart.

"It's nothing serious," he told Herman Skunk. "She probably fainted from the heat and the recent stress. A couple days of bed rest will do her good," he said guiding him to his cart.

"Is there something you can give her?" Herman Skunk asked.

"We all are under a lot of stress and there is no medicine that can cure it, except for rest."

"She hasn't been herself lately, especially since our son was inducted into the army. She's afraid he will die."

"It has been a year Herman and there hasn't been any war declared nor any violence from the town's people. I think the king was angry and wanted to flaunt his power."

Herman looked at the doctor but did not comment.

"You have to admit that he has done great improvement. The school has been enlarged and much needed books are in the classrooms. We have ten students enrolled in the newly formed college that is now meeting in the old mansion and fifty more have registered for next year. The construction of the new college will be completed by then. Our children no longer have to go to other towns just to get a higher education. Our dirt streets have been paved. The king has made lots of improvements that benefit the entire community."

"He has made improvements with out money," the doctor said in a huff.

"At least we see where our money is going. With his father, he spent the entire treasure on himself and his family."

"King John was a loveable king."

"Yes, he was loveable but he didn't care about the citizens."

"We were happier. Laughter was in the land."

"We were happier, but the town was slowly turning into a ghost town. Now the town has a new coat of paint. Building that were decaying and falling apart, have been torn down and new ones constructed."

"But there's no laughter. Everyone is sad and depressed."

"Yes they are. If only the king didn't raise the taxes so high."

"Yes," Dr. Raccoon said climbing up into his wagon. "Herman don't worry about your wife, we will look after her until all the festivities have ended."

Herman looked in the back of the cart, Dr. Raccoon's wife was sitting next to his wife, sponging her forehead. Sharon's eyes were opened but they looked so empty.

"Go," the doctor said. "Don't worry. When you have finished here, come by the house and take your wife home."

When the king called out his name, David was as surprised as the animals. He surely thought the king would make the same challenge as before, but this time he would not volunteer. And now the king had called out his name in challenge.

As David looked around, he saw the animals glared at him with animosity in their eyes. They dared him to win the race.

Coming forward, David took his position at the starting line and waited for the signal.

The race stared out as before. The king sped by him, leaving him in the wake of his dust.

Once again the king allowed other things to distract his mind. He stopped and played with the butterflies, bees and took a short nap. When he thought the tortoise was near the finish line, he raced at top speed, knowing that he was first across the line.

When the king came around the bend, he was surprised to see that David was securely across the finished line. This time there was no crowd there to watch his defeat.

When the animals saw David coming around the bend and the king was nowhere in sight, they lost hope and went home, leaving only Herman Skunk to report the defeat.

Herman looked at David and the king and shook his head. He was tired and was in a hurry to see his wife. There will not be much to print tomorrow in the newspaper. He had to think of something to write by tomorrow for the morning news edition.

Herman Skunk took his wife home but she never recovered and a month later she died. It was a sad time for the Skunk's family. The doctor did all he could but she refused to live.

The next two years was a repeat of the king's defeat. Saul was beside himself. Each year his defeat had became more humiliating. The last time he came around the bend no one was in sight. He thought he had won but as he neared the finished line, he saw David a forth-of-a-mile away. He had crossed the finished line and was on his way home. *This could not be*, he thought, unless David had a secret weapon. There was no other possible reason that a slow moving creature could win against him. It was just impossible.

Hour after hour Saul pondered about his constant defeats. There was no possible reason for him to loose the foot race.

Standing before the mirror, he took note of his sleek muscular body. He had a large head and a large head housed a large brain and a larger brain housed a more intelligent mind. His head was three times larger than David. So why did he continue to lose the foot race against David?

Next he observed his body. He had a long sleek, muscular body and legs, a guarantee of speed. David had a short round body and stubby legs a guarantee to loose. It takes a tortoise much longer to get from one destination to another. The mirror and logic has proved that his body is more superior.

So what… suddenly it dawned on him. It's the shell. David carried a shell on his back. That has to be the reason he has been able to win the races. Why didn't he think of this earlier? Saul laughed out loud. So David thought he could put one over him. He now knows he has a secret. He didn't know where David was hiding it, but once he found it he would expose him before everyone.

Saul laughed and laughed as he prepared for bed. Yes, David was a sly one but not anymore. No sir, he was going to get to the bottom of his deceit and there he will find his secret.

Once he was exposed, his subjects would sing praises to his name. Marching around the room he began singing.

"Hurrah! Hurrah! Hurrah!
Saul is the winner!
Saul is the winner!
Hurrah! Hurrah!
He has defeated the David
the slowest tortoise in the land!
Hurrah! Hurrah!

The next day, Saul's top priority was spying on David, watching his every move. The vision that kept running though his mind was of David surprise when he exposed him for cheating. Then Thelma Beaver would come up to him and put a ribbon around his neck and kiss him. He couldn't count the number of times he had fantasized about her. This was his secret fantasy, a kiss from Thelma Beaver. Such thoughts danced over and over in his mind as a slow smile surfaced on his face.

He recalled the first time he laid eyes on her. It was at the crowning of the Queen of Summer. There were many contestants and he didn't notice them until she began to sing. It was the most beautiful voice he had ever heard. She took his breath away. Dressed in a soft pink gown, she looked like a princess. At that very moment he fell in love with her.

Whenever he was around her his heart would beat so loud that he couldn't hear anything. Butterflies fluttered in his stomach and his legs grew weak. He would break out in a cold sweat and large lumps formed in his throat. He had it bad but he didn't know what to do about it. When she stood before him with her hand extended toward him, he had no idea what possessed him to kiss her hand or why the small jester made his heart beat loudly in his chest. Only when she started withdrawing her hand that he released it. He sat like an idiot staring at her. He could not help himself because he knew that she had his heart in her hand and though she didn't even know it.

He couldn't let her go as he led her to the dance floor. For a few glorious minutes, he held the woman he loved in his arms. He didn't see or hear anyone, only the sights of her beautiful face.

He was so fascinated with her that he had a throne, similar to his, upholstered in pink satin similar erected next to his throne. He had a crown made that was similar to her tiara with precious stones circling it. A cape of white and pink fur was sewed and now it hung in a display case along with the crown. His subjects had thought he had chosen a bride when he had the throne, cape and crown prepared but after several years, they realized that it was another one of his phases. They had hoped he would marry and maybe then his behavior would change.

Returning his mind to spying, he concluded that spying was boring. David was a tortoise of habit. At sunrise, he ate his meager breakfast of bugs, bread and milk. Afterward, he would leave his house with a backpack strap on his back. It seemed like eternity before he reached the bank of the river that was near his house.

When he finally reached the bank, he would get into the boat, throw out the fishing net, start the engine of the boat and ride across the river. When the net was full he'll drag his load to shore. By that time Gregg Fox and his two sons were waiting with their wagon. After the catch was loaded into the cart, the Foxes rode into town.

David's prosperity at fishing was strange to Saul because others had tried to make a living fishing, but David was the only one that was successful. This confirmed Saul's belief that the tortoise possessed some magical or mystical powers.

After Gregg Fox and his sons left with their wagon loaded, the sun was high in the sky. Instead of returning home, David would leisurely gather his fishing pole and throw a line in the water and wait for a minnow to bite. Once again David displayed unusual behavior. Saul wondered why he didn't keep any of the fish that were loaded onto Gregg Fox's wagon? Instead he sat on the bank casting a line for a fish. His behavior was quite puzzling.

After throwing his line into the water, David would secure his pole under a large rock, reach into his little bag and take out his lunch and slowly began to eat. After lunch, he would pull his line in with his one small fish and slowly walk into town.

At the market place, he bought chunks of fruits, vegetables, bread and other goods for his dinner. He spoke quietly and briefly. He was a quiet and reserved animal. It was the same exchange each day, in the same manner and actions. Finishing his purchase, he would walk slowly down the road back to his cottage.

After several days of watching David, Saul became bored. He knew David had a secret beneath his shell but he was unable to find what it was.

He knew David was hiding his secret beneath the shell but in all his spying he had not found one lead.

One day as Saul was sitting on a hill watching David fish, his eyes focused on the shell on his back. Suddenly everything became clear. It's the shell! The shell on David's back is where he keeps his secrets. Why didn't he see this before! No reason he hasn't been able to discover the secret.

When he followed David, he only saw him mostly from the back. This gave David ample opportunity to pull out his secret weapon unaware by him.

He jumped up rejoicing and ran back to the castle. He was delighted that he no longer had to follow the slow tortoise around.

In his study, he sat down at his desk and began constructing a plan and listed all the materials he needed. In a couple of hours he was able to gather all the supplies he needed except for the tortoise shell. He couldn't just walk in the mercantile and request a tortoise shell or go to the cemetery and dig up one. So he deiced to search the countryside for one. For days he searched high and low for an empty tortoise shell, but none was found.

He had almost given up until one afternoon he saw a small hill in the middle of a clearing covered with dense foliage. He started to walk away until he spied something orange peering out of the dense foliage. Coming closer to investigate, he saw that it wasn't a hill but something hidden beneath the dead grass, derbies and weeds. Clearing away the debris, Saul discovered that it was large, round with bright yellow and orange colors and a few dots of red. To his surprise, it was a tortoise shell. Picking up the shell, he was amazed that the shell was not heavy but light and almost transparent. Turning the shell over; he discovered that a skeleton laid beneath it. The poor fellow must have been in a fight, Saul concluded by the marks on the shell or he was just old and couldn't go any further.

Picking up the shell, he inspected it more closely. He was amazed how light the shell was. He had thought it would be heavy. The bone skeleton that lay beneath it was small, so there had to be secret compartments that disappeared when they die. He sat the shell down and covered the skeleton remains with dirt and derbies that was around the shell.

"How could such a shell conceal a secret weapon?" he asked. He could not come up with a straight answer, but was confident that when he reached the castle he would discover all he needed to know. With a smile of victory on his face, he skipped happily down the road with the shell in tow.

He hid the shell near the castle and waited until it was dark before sneaking it into the castle beneath several gray blankets.

The next day while the king was busy with his new-found discovery, the mayor called a special meeting to discuss what they should do about the race that was to start in one week. Since the king continued to lose the foot races against David, he made their lives miserable. Laughter had left the land. Everyone was afraid the soldiers would come to their home and confiscate their property as they had done to several families. Not only that, the soldiers had free reign and sometimes they imposed harsh punishment on the animals for no reason. The taxes had increased from ten to fifteen percent, the food and goods had doubled in price. It was a dark day for the animals of the forest.

They felt that if David won the race again, the king would impose even harsher punishments. The main thing that puzzled the animals was why did the king continued to lose the foot race each year? Everyone knew the king was the fastest animal around. Yet each year, he would lose the foot race to the slowest animal in the forest? There was another question they pondered, why did the king linger in the forest. Was he meeting someone? What was distracting the king from continuing with the race?

"We should demand that David not race," Willie Tortoise said in frustration. Taking off his white baseball hat, he ran his hand over his bald spot and replaced the cap on his head. Whenever Otter Beaver became upset or nervous, he would repeat this ritual. Some wondered was that the reason he had no hair on the top of his head.

"I agree," said his brother Adam setting into a chair near the mayor's desk. Leaned back he propped his legs on the desk and crossed them. "We have been working from sun up to sun down each day just to pay our taxes. When we think we're ahead it's time to pay the next one."

"We could cancel the celebration."

"We tried once to cancel the celebration and the king was furious. And you remember that he made a law that everyone must be present for the celebration," said Ralph Hare the father of Jessie Hare, who teased David. He was so irate that he bit his nails out of frustration.

"Celebration!" Anne Chipmunk said pacing back and forth. "What's to celebrate but another year of misery!"

"I never had nightmares but as the celebration… ugh event draws closer, I keep seeing the king as tall as the great tree with a spear in his hand commanding the army to attack and kill all of us," said Horace Ferret.

"You should stop eating so much spicy food," Otter said with a smile on his face.

"I haven't been about to eat spicy food for the past year."

"None of us have been eating or doing things we normally do because of the king."

"If we could predict the king's mood we would know what to do," Horace said.

"That's not impossible. We know the king will be in a foul mood as usual. What we need to do is to find a way to prevent David from racing against the king," Otter said wiping his tired eyes. He didn't want to admit to the group that he too had been having problem sleeping. He was afraid not only for his family, but for his two sons in the king's army. They seemed so hard and distant. Rarely were they allowed to come home and when they did it was only for a couple of hours.

"We could talk to David and reason with him," Otter Beaver said.

"He has to know our perils and besides what can he do. Refuse to show for the race?" said Anna Chipmunk ringing her hands in front of her.

"Yes you're right. We're right back to where we started," said Nathan Otter the owner of the mercantile. "If the animals do not start buying more of my merchandise, I'll go broke," he said, his eyes wide with desperation.

"You're not the only one loosing money," Anna Chipmunk the owner of the bakery said wiping some flowers from her apron. In her rush to leave the shop she forgot to remove her apron and take the hair net off her head.

"We could ask the king's family again."

"No, that won't work. I have talked to his family and they will have nothing to do with him. Since Saul came to power, they have no influence over him. The first thing he did was to cut their ration of food and they were not allowed to purchase any new clothing," the mayor said shaking his head. "All the fancy clothes and parties they used to have were denied to them. That was quite a blow to his mother's ego. She was so angry and frustrated that she went to live with her brother after she was able to get her daughters married."

"That was a cruel blow to the family, wasn't it?"

"Yes it was. Marinade had big plans for her two daughters from birth. She had always boasted that they would marry only royalty but instead they married poor merchants," said Annie Chipmunk shaking her head.

"From what I heard, she was lucky to find anyone who wanted to marry her penniless daughters."

"I would not want that to happen to my daughters."

"If they had a dowry they could have rich husbands, but their brother only gave them a small dowry."

"I heard through the grapevine that the family is broke," the mayor said.

"This can't be true. All the tax money they collected from us. No way."

"That's right. Saul is just frugal and unwilling to let to go of a cent."

"Now is not the time to talk about our frugal king. What we came here to discuss is how can we keep David from attending the celebration and making our lives a living hell!"

"We could post a guard around his house, preventing him from leaving," suggested Henry Red Tail Squirrel.

They stared in disbelief at Henry as he made such a ridiculous suggestion. There are times when he was nuttier than the nuts he sold in his store.

"Henry, where have you been? Better yet, have you been listening to a word we have been saying?" asked the mayor with frustration in his voice.

"At least it's a suggestion," he said in defense.

The mayor shook his head as he walked to the window and peered left and right. He had become suspicious that someone was feeding the king information regarding their meetings.

He knew if they were observed meeting, they all could be labeled traitors and sent to jail. On the street there was only a handful of people going about their business. Years ago the street would have been full of happy people as they crowded the streets shopping. Children laughed and happily played with each other as their parents shopped or talked to their friends, but now most of the animals lived in fear.

"What are we to do?" Mayor Samuel said turning from the window with fear in his eyes.

"We could bribe him," Anna suggested.

Adam was about to speak but instead he leaned forward in the chair and looked at each one of them.

"With what? David has everything he needs," Eli Tortoise said. "He's not rich but he makes a comfortable living."

"We could bribe him with your daughter," Otter Beaver said laughing. They would have laughed at the fatalistic attempt at humor, but given the circumstances they only shook their head.

"That's not funny. Besides my daughter is engaged to marry Terry Tortoise in a few weeks."

"This is not a joking matter," the mayor said. "Does anyone have any sensible suggestions?"

"What are we to do?" Anna asked, twisting her apron between her hands as she prowled the room, pausing to wipe an imaginary spot of dust from the desk.

When she heard no response, she turned and saw that the mayor had returned to staring out the window. She wished he wouldn't do that. He made her so nervous. Sometimes she thought the soldiers would burst through the door and arrest them.

After the silence continued, the mayor turned and looked at the group. They all were staring at him for an answer. He didn't have one and he didn't know how they were going to solve their predicament.

Becoming tired of the bickering, the mayor's wife spoke up. "Why should we approach David with such ridiculous schemes and run the of risk going to jail. The king is bigger, taller, stronger and faster than David and if the king wants to make a complete fool of himself each year, let him. If he would concentrate on the race, there is no way he could loose."

Everyone looked at her with surprise written on each face. The mayor opened his mouth to speak but nothing came out. They all knew what she had said was the truth. There was no way a tortoise could win against a hare!

"You're right," the major said in defeat. "There is nothing we can do but hope that the king wins the race."

One by one they each left the office with their head lowered in defeat, dispensing to their homes and businesses. There wasn't anything anyone could do to prevent the disaster that was forthcoming.

The day of the festival was not a happy one for the animals. They didn't rush to the clearing as they did in the past, nor did they welcome each other. In the past, they had up to twenty-five floats, several marching bands and twenty clowns. This year they had only ten floats, no band and no clowns.

Very little work went into the celebration. No one was happy. They sat around with frowns and sad faces. Even the mayor didn't make an elaborate speech.

While the animals were down-hearted, King Saul was in high spirits as always. He was happy on this occasion because he had found David's secret weapon and today he would be the winner.

At the start of the race, the crowd assembled around with sadness and dread written all over their faces. Over the years they had learned not to put their faith in the king to win the race.

David took his place at the starting line as usual. Over the years he had learned not to wait until Saul made the challenge. As he stood at the starting line, he looked around and saw the animals glaring angrily at him, hoping he would deliberately lose the race. David was sympathetic to their concerns and felt that if he accidentally lost the race, then Saul would be happy and no longer punish the animals. This went against his belief, but the animals were his family and friends.

Saul feeling very confident did not share the animals' concerns. He disappeared into the thickets and emerged with his secret weapon.

The animals stopped what they were doing as a hush settled over the entire crowd. They stood gawking at the king with the strange thing in his hands emerging from the thickets.

"It's a tortoise shell," someone whispered.

"What is he going to do with it?"

Saul had the animals' full attention as they stared with their mouths gaping staring at him. When he hoisted the shell up on his back and began to strap and tie the shell around his body with wires and ropes, not an animal moved.

In all of their lives they had never seen such a stupid contraction. With the shell on his back their king looked utterly ridiculous. They looked at one another in bewilderment. They could not believe what they saw. Now they knew without a doubt that the king had truly lost his mind.

One of the younger children looked up at her mother and asked, "What is that, mother."

"Shhhhh," her mother said as she too tried to understand why the king had an empty tortoise shell strapped to his back. Everyone was to frightened to ask the question out loud. No one uttered a word.

David, filled with astonishment and surprise, stared at the king with his mouth open. Mouth opened, he tried to speak, but nothing came out. What could he say? When the king first revealed the shell, David thought he was making fun of him and felt a tinge of hostility. But the feeling diminished when the king began to secure the shell around his body. Then he knew it was not a joke.

The animals thought their king was strange and today they knew it.

It took several minutes for the king to secure the shell tightly around his body with the ropes, wires and fasteners. The fasteners were tighter than he anticipated but he hoped that as he walked they would loosen.

Satisfied that the shell was secured, he began to walk back and forth in front of David. Closing his mouth, David began to laugh inside at the ridiculous sight before him. *Why would the king want to strap an empty tortoise shell to his back?* he wondered. He had to close his eyes and concentrate to keep from laughing out loud.

The king noticing the surprise on David's face smiled with gratification. Today was the day he would defeat the slow moving tortoise and everyone would shout his name in victory!.

The countdown of the race began. Saul took the lead but began to slow down when the ropes securing the shell around his body began to loosen. A couple of them came unfastened tangling around his long limbs. He tried to tighten the restraints that came unfastened too, but before he could tighten them, the shell shifted and several other restraints loosen. The more he tried to secure the shell the more it swayed from side to side until it fell between his legs causing him to lose his balance. The king ended up lying flat on his back inside the shell. The more he tried to free his body the more entangled he became and tighter the ropes and wires became digging into his flesh.

The king was using words that he didn't know he knew. He was so frustrated that he didn't know how to free himself from his predicament. He would have cried if it would help him to free his body. His embarrassment was hard enough to stomach let alone crying like a small child.

All too late the king knew his error. He had drawn up the plans but he failed to try it out before the race. Now there he lay upside down in the tortoise shell utterly embarrassed. He didn't know what looked stupider, him loosing the foot race to a slow tortoise or lying upside down in this stupid shell. The latter one was more embarrassing.

The animals didn't know what to do. They wanted to assist the king but they felt that he would not accept their help, especially in such a ridiculous predicament.

The mayor decided that he had to do something so he hesitantly walked up to the king, trying to scrutinize the best way to free the king. Catching the shell on the side, he was able to set the king upright after several tries.

Standing upright, the king was so angry that he shoved the mayor aside, knocking both of them off balance. Once again Saul ended up on his back, within the shell, and the mayor was lying on the ground beside him. The king shouted words of scorn at the mayor as he tried in vain to release the constraints. Gaining his feet, the mayor moved away from Saul at a fast pace.

When Saul realized he wasn't able to free himself from the restraints, he shouted to the captain to assist him. Confused by what he saw, the captain was hesitant in coming to his aid. He took several steps and halted before he ran to the king's aid.

The animals knew that their hope of victory was lost and the king would once again lose the race. They gathered up their possessions and families and quickly went to their homes before the soldiers were ordered to disperse them.

The captain tried to free the king, but there were so many ropes and wires that he was having a difficult time. When he thought he was making progress, he slipped and became entangled with the king. He then ended up sitting in the king's lap with the ropes holding him securely. The more they struggled the tighter the restraints became. Saul was so entrapped that he had trouble breathing especially with the captain sitting in his lap. Their sight was so comical that the soldiers began to snicker. This infuriated the king as he struck the captain over and over.

"Move you clumsy morons!" the king shouted as he tried to push the captain off of him.

"Don't just stand there, Justin," the captain shouted to the second in command. "Come over here and help us!" he shouted.

"Sorry sir," Justin said coming to their rescue.

"Get us out of this contraction!" the captain shouted.

"I'm trying sir but there are so many ropes and wires that it's hard for me to find the right one."

Justin pulled a knife from his pocket and tried to cut part of the rope that confined them but the rope was too large for his little knife. He was having a difficult time because of the king's constant movements. After some time and several nicks and cuts to his arms, he was able to cut the ropes free, but he had nothing to cut the metal wires.

One of the soldiers had to run to the blacksmith shop to get some wire-cutters. So the king and the captain could do nothing buy lie in the upside down shell, feeling humiliated.

By the time the soldier returned and freed the two, the hour was late. David had run down to Mrs. Snail's house and returned. When he was near the finish-line, he could see that the king still confided to the contraption strapped to his back with the captain lying in his lap.

When the last wire was cut, David was near the finish-line. Instead of crossing, he turned watching the excitement.

Once the king was freed he limped over to the throne. His clothes were torn and he had several nicks and cuts on his body. He had so many emotions running through his body, he didn't know how to react, so he said nothing. The soldiers hoisted the wooden throne on their shoulders and hurried down the road to the castle. In their wake they left pieces of ropes, screws and twisted wires all over the ground.

David shook his head and began to laugh out loud as he visualized the king with the shell strapped around his body. He laughed so hard and long that tears rolled down his face as he fell to the ground holding his stomach. Every time he looked at the shell, his laughter would start anew. It was some time before he was able to contain himself. Wiping the tears from his face, he got up from the ground and slowly walked home. Tomorrow he would meet with the king about his friends. He must make the king see that the foot races were only a game.

Safely at home, David sat in his comfortable chair eating a slice of Mrs. Squirrel's pecan pie, still amused at the memory of the king with the stupid shell strapped on his back. Finishing the pie, he nestled back farther in the chair, listening to his stereo.

True to his word, David went before the secretary to get an audience with the king the very next day. He paid his fee and waited. A few minutes later the secretary returned. The king refused to see him and his money was returned. For three days he tried and three times his money was returned. With no other recourse, he forsook trying to get an audience with the king.

As the king sat on his throne, he pondered why he had lost the foot race. There was no way he should have lost the foot race. He was faster and smarter than all the other animals in the forest, yet he could not win a foot race against the slowest creature in the forest. How could he lose when everything was in his favor? He thought he had the tortoise's secret weapon and that should have guaranteed him victory, but instead he was humiliated. Then he thought, maybe it was not the shell. Could it be something higher? If it was something higher, he didn't know what it could be.

"No," he said, shaking his head. He surmised that it was not something higher. It's the shell. Yet he hadn't found the answer and he probably never would. He concluded that he would never be able to defeat David in a foot race. The foot race started out as a joke but the joke backfired and now he was the target of the joke. He knew his subjects were laughing behind his back. He would too if he wasn't so embarrassed. The highlight came when he strapped that shell on his back and ended upside down. He had provided the crowd with amusement for the rest of the year. He was so embarrassed that he rarely went out in public. He was the king, the animals were to respect him not laugh and whisper behind his back.

Even though the newspaper reported that neither animal crossed the finish-line, the animals snubbed David. They treated him like the plague.

The mayor was angry about the foot race. He called a meeting and the group decided to boycott fish. It was unanimously concluded that once David saw that the animals were not going to buy fish, with the loss of customers, David would be penniless and hopefully disheartened and leave their town forever. Satisfied that they had a flawless plan, the group carried out their plan the very next day.

Word soon circulated that no one was to purchase fish. Many of the animals complied with the boycott and did not purchase fish while others who thought it was a stupid idea continued to purchase fish. Those who did not comply with the boycott could not prevent the tragedy. The odor of dead and rotten fish began to permeate as they piled up at the market-place. After four days of boycotting, David did not venture out in his boat. The town reeked from the prudent smell of rotting fish.

No one noticed that David no longer continued his daily trip into town to purchase his daily meals except for Herman Skunk. He felt that something should be done so he wrote three articles in his newspaper regarding the five wealthiest families in town.

The fifth wealthiest family: Mayor Thomas D. Beaver. Mayor Thomas owned several rental properties.

The fourth wealthiest family: Red Tail Squirrel. Red Tail owns the sawmill, furniture and mercantile stores in the surrounding towns.

The mayor was outraged that he was not the wealthiest family in the town but the fifth. The bad news hurt his ego. He was so angry that he would not leave his house the whole day.

The second day when Herman Skunk opened the door, there were about fifteen animals who had gathered outside the door, waiting to learn who was the second and third wealthiest family. Not to disappoint his readers, Herman Skunk printed the article and the animals were once again amazed.

***The third wealthiest family*: the Otter family. The Otter's owned the grain mill and a fleet of ships.**

The second wealthiest family: the Beaver family. The Beaver's who owned the only construction company and half of the buildings in town.

On the third day a large crowd had gathered outside the newspapers waiting in anticipation to see who was the wealthiest family in town. To meet the demand, Herman Skunk and his family had worked all night just to have enough newspapers for the masses.

On the front of the paper in large bold letters was written:

"DAVID TORTOISE, THE RICHES ANIMAL IN TOWN"

The story told about his life and wealth. Being a practical tortoise, David bought stocks in several businesses in the surrounding towns. The animals were shocked to learn that David's, the smallest tortoise, wealth far exceeded the other four families combined. All this time the town's inhabitants had thought David was poor and was barely making a living. The animals, especially the mayor, realized their follies and immediately lifted the boycott.

The next day, a group of citizens went to the market place expecting to buy fish but when they arrived they discovered that the market-place was deserted. Gregg Fox and his family were nowhere in sight and the only fish to be purchased was from Sly Weasel. Weasel's clothes were tattered and dirty, and his body had a smell that was worse than the fish. The price he charged per fish was three times higher than what the Foxes charged for four.

Refusing to buy from Sly Weasel and the mayor leading the way, the citizens went to Gregg Fox's home and wanted to know why he hadn't brought any fish to town, but he wasn't home. His wife informed them that he was down at the river.

So the group went down to the river to confront Gregg Fox. They found him sitting on the dock fishing. When he saw them coming, he pointed over to the dock where David's boat should be. They looked up and down the river but the boat was nowhere in sight.

"Gregg Fox," the mayor called angrily. "Why haven't you brought any fish to the market place?"

Gregg Fox sat at the riverbank casting his line into the water. He was a man who did not rush, no matter what happened. Once his line was cast to his satisfaction, he turned and looks directly at the mayor.

"No fish," was all he said as he turned and directed his attention back to his cast line.

"What do you mean no fish?" the mayor asked becoming frustrated.

"Just what I said mayor. No fish," he replied not looking around.

"Why isn't there any fish?"

"No David," Gregg Fox.

"You are trying my patience Gregg Fox! I wish you would speak in plain English so we all can understand what you are saying," the mayor said shaking his head as he paced back and forth. Stopping he turned and faced Gregg Fox.

"I can see that David has taken out his boat. So where is your cart to hall his load to town?"

"No cart because of the boycott."

"The boycott is over, haven't you heard?"

"Nobody told David." Gregg Fox shook his head as pulled in his catch. He took the fish from the hook and added it to the bucket that already had several fishes in it.

Becoming frustrated, Anna Chipmunk approached Gregg Fox. "Where is David?" she asked.

"Gone."

"I can see that David is gone. Gone where?"

"Don't know."

"Isn't he fishing?"

"Don't know."

"Do you know anything, Gregg Fox?" the mayor shouted out of frustration.

"Nope," he said casting his line back into the river.

"We can see that David's boat is not here. And you said you don't know if he's fishing. When was the last time you saw David?" Eli Tortoise asked hoping to get a straight answer.

"Oh, I say about five or six days ago."

"What!" Eli cried.

The mayor pushed Eli out of the way as he came up to Gregg Fox.

Standing beside Gregg Fox, the mayor spoke. "Man, are you telling me that David has been missing for five days?"

"I didn't say he was missing, mayor. I said I have not seen him for five or six days," Gregg Fox said correcting the mayor. "Could be longer," he added with a smirk on his face.

"What about the boat?"

Gregg looked at the mayor and shook his head. "I guess he took it with him when he left."

The crowd began to murmur among themselves as they looked out on the empty river. David was gone and no one knew where he went.

"Did he by any chance tell you where he was going?" Anne Chipmunk asked pushing the mayor aside, almost knocking him into the lake.

"I don't rightly know. He doesn't tell me his every move."

"Why didn't you ask him?" Anne screamed. "Gregg Fox, answer me!"

Gregg Fox reeled in his line, carefully packed up his gear and walked away from the crowd. As far as he was concerned, he had answered their questions and yet they still wanted more. It's their entire fault for boycotting David and now that they have read in the newspaper about him being the wealthiest man in town, they expected him to appear out of thin air. Gregg Fox wasn't surprised about what the newspaper said about David being a rich tortoise. He knew David was a very thrifty tortoise. He wasn't like his family who spent every penny they made and are penniless.

Three days later David's boat appeared in the river. He was bewildered to see the riverbank crowded with animals. As he neared the dock, a loud cheer went out. Such a welcome was not something he had anticipated nor did he want to see. The last time they cheered him, the king imposed harsh laws and they blamed him. He could turn around and head back to the sea, but he was tired and he missed his warm comfortable home.

As he came within hearing distance, they all began to talk at once. He could not understand what they were talking about, so he just stood and stared at them, as some of the men assisted in anchoring his boat to the dock.

The mayor stood in front of the group with a bright smile on his face. David immediately knew something was wrong. The mayor hated him and blamed him for all of their problems.

Nearing the boat, he spoke. "David we are so glad to see you." The crowd nodded their heads with smiles on their faces.

"We hope you had a wonderful vacation. You look rested," he said with the smile still on his face.

"Mayor will you get down to business," someone shouted from the crowd.

Turning, the mayor put up both hands. "I'm getting to that." Returning his attending to David, he continued, "We are glad you're back. And now that you're back, we hope you will begin fishing right away. We have missed tasting those tasty fish," he said licking his lips.

David didn't reply nor did he smile. When he learned that the mayor had organized the merchants and encouraged the whole town to restrain from buying fish, he was devastated. At first he hoped it was a phase and after a day without fish, they would see that such a boycott was futile. When he went into town the fourth day and saw that only a handful bought fish, he went home and packed up his boat and went out to sea searching for a new home. While he was there, he was able to relax and see that his anger did not solve anything. If the animals didn't want to purchase fish, he was helpless in making them. Now the same business leaders who encouraged the animals not to purchase fish were standing before him with smiles on their face hoping he would continue fishing.

He alighted from the boat and made sure it was secured before he walked away.

"David?" the mayor said following behind him.

He stopped and turned around, facing the mayor.

"Did you hear what I had said that we're sorry," the mayor said still smiling.

"I heard everything you had said mayor and I will consider what you have said." He turned and continued walking.

"David," the mayor said approaching him. He turned around and looked at the mayor.

"The wife and I would like to invite you to dinner. We have invited a few friends over and we thought you would like to attend. I know this is kind of sudden, but I have been meaning to invite you over for a long time."

David was concerned about the mayor's sudden change of heart. He had never invited him to have a cup of tea with him let alone a meal. This puzzled David and he wondered what had conspired while he was away. Years ago he would have jumped at such a chance to have dinner with the mayor and the prominent animals of the town, but that was in the past.

"I'm busy," David said as he turned and continued walking.

The mayor stood with his mouth open. He was surprised at David's reaction. The crowd was not happy either as they returned to their homes.

The next day Gregg Fox along with his sons went down to the river at the usual time, expecting to see David coming to shore with his catch of fish. The boat was docked in the same position as yesterday and David was nowhere in sight. Returning to the cart, Gregg Fox went into town.

When he reached the market-place, there was a crowd of people waiting for him. When they saw his cart empty, they swarm around him all talking at one.

"Everyone please be quiet," Gregg Fox shouted. "I'm sorry there are no fish. David did not go out today. Maybe tomorrow."

"Mayor didn't you apologize to David?" Henry Red Tail Squirrel asked.

The mayor coming forward spoke. "Of course I apologized to David. You all heard me," he said looking at the animals for support. They all nodded their heads

"Well what did he say."

"He said he'll think about it."

"What's there to think about?" Anna Chipmunk asked as she nervously pulled at her apron.

"Yeah," they shouted.

"It's all your fault mayor. If you hadn't come up with the stupid idea to boycott David none of this would had happened," Wendy Possum said clutching her twins to her chest.

"Yeah," they shouted.

"If we want fish we have to go to Sly Weasel and he charges four times what we normally pay for a small fish!" Billy Raccoon shouted.

"It's all your fault mayor," someone else shouted as the crowd began to converge on him.

"Wait a minute. It's not my fault," the mayor said backing up. He was afraid that the crowd would cause him great ham. "Don't blame me," he begged.

"It is your fault. If you hadn't come up with a ridiculous boycott scheme none of this would have happened!" Gregg Fox said standing before the mayor. Gregg Fox who rarely talked and never in history had he ever raised his voice, but today he was angry and shouting at the mayor. "David is our friend and he never did anything wrong to us. Because of that stupid foot race, everyone blamed David for winning, especially you," he said pointing a finger at the mayor's chest. "All his life he has been treated as an outsider. If it wasn't for Herman Skunk printing that story about how rich and valuable David is to this town, no one would have apologized."

Turning his attention from the mayor, Gregg Fox focused his attention on the crowd. "All David is guilty of is trying to fit in. Everything he did, you laughed at him and called him names because of his size. You all should be ashamed of the way you have treated him. You have forgotten that he has feelings too."

The crowd hung their heads in shame. There was nothing they could say. In the back of the crowd David stood, hearing everything that was said. Now he understood why the mayor was so nice to him. He had come into town to accept the major's offer for dinner but now after hearing what he said, he turned and went back home.

"Gregg Fox, I don't like what you said," the mayor said angrily.

The crowd turned and looked at the two.

"You try to blame me for everything and that's not true."

"Not true! Not true!" he said coming eye to eye with the mayor. "For someone that was never elected to be our spokesperson you have stuck your fat oversized body in everyone's businesses. You flaunt your money before our faces and now you have learned that you are not as rich as David. Now you want to be his friend!" Gregg Fox shouted jabbing the mayor's chest with his finger.

"Everyone knows how friendly I am. I am friends to everyone," the mayor said trying to avoid Gregg Fox.

"You are only a friend to those who have money and your only concern is how to make more. Well your plan backfired and now the whole town must suffer for your stupidity."

The mayor opened his mouth to speak, but when he looked at the crowd and saw the anger written on their faces, he didn't speak. He was ashamed and afraid.

Gregg Fox was so angry that he turned and walked away. He was fearful that if he stayed a minute longer he would punch the mayor right in his fat face.

The next day Gregg Fox and his sons went down to the river as usual. They were happy to see David with a large catch of fish in his net. No words were spoken none were needed.

As the months passed and summer gave way to winter, the animals were well-stocked with fish and nestled warm in their homes. Then winter came and went and the snow melted. The land was reborn as the green grass sprouted up between the brown dead grass of the past year. The tree limbs budded and new branches and leaves decorated the bare trees. With spring in the air birds returned to the valley and began to raise a new family. Everything was green and colorful.

As the ice melted off the river, David began his fishing once again. Today as usual he helped Gregg Fox and his sons pull in a net full of fish into the cart. Looking up David saw an angel standing a few feet from them. He blinked several times as if he couldn't believe his eyes. His jaw dropped as he gasped at the angel dressed in a pale green gown with a smile that made his world turn upside down. He never saw anyone so beautiful.

Instantly he lost his heart to the angel. He was so intrigued with her that he wasn't paying attention to what he was doing or going. All thumbs, he grabbed for the net but instead of the net, he grabbed Jack's shirt and stepped on his foot. This move caused him to crash into Jack knocking both backward. Trying to correct their balance, they both released their hold on the net, freeing some of the fishes; dumping them on them. They were covered with wiggling, smelly fishes as they tried to reach the water.

Annetta watched the mishap and clamped her hand over her mouth to keep from laughing out loud. She quickly recovered, rushed over and helped Mr. Fox and his eldest son recover the flapping fish that tried to make their way back to the water.

"David, what's wrong with you," Jack Fox screamed as he pushed David off him along with the fish.

"I lost my heart," he mumbled to himself as he gained his feet.

"Sorry," David said out aloud helping Jack to his feet.

Gregg Fox smiled as he observed David.

"If you two are finished playing, you can give us a hand," Mr. Fox said holding a squirming fish in his hand.

It took half an hour to rescue the fish that escaped from the net. When all the fish were in the cart, Mr. Fox bid them a good day and drove down the road with a smile on his face.

"Paw, what's so funny," his youngest son, asked looking at him strangely.

"Life my boy," he said laughing out loud. His son looked at David and then his father. He could not understand what was going on. His father turned and looked at David, his brother who sat next to him was smiling as if he had swallowed a frog. Mr. Fox realizing his son did not understand what was so funny, bent over and he whispered something in his ear. Jack turned in the seat and looked at David with his mouth open and suddenly, he too burst out laughing.

"Hi, my name is Annetta. My family just moved in the old house on the other side of Tina Snail's house," she said extending her hand.

David looked at the extended hand and was very afraid. Hesitantly he grasped her hand and retrieved it as quickly.

"My name is David."

"David you live around here?"

"Uh hum," was all he was able to say.

"You catch fish for a living?"

"Uh hum."

"I like fish."

David didn't answer but continued to stare at her. He didn't know why except she was so beautiful.

"Is this your backpack?"

He nodded.

She opened it and pulled out two slices of beard, some fruit and two green leaves.

"I'm hungry. Is it okay if I share your lunch?" she asked sitting on a large rock near the bank.

David nodded his head.

"You don't say very much, do you?"

He shook his head in reply.

"Come and sit by me," she said patting the stone near her. David looked at her hand and then her face. He didn't know what to do. She looked at him with a bright smile and continued patting the stone near her until he walked over and sat down, his eyes never leaving her face.

She gave him his fishing pole as she prepared their lunch. For the next hour Annitta did all the talking and David fished. Instead of his usual one fish, he caught six. He was so preoccupied with Annitta that he had problems concentrating. When he saw the six fish, he didn't know what to do. He would have continued fishing if she hadn't taken the fishing pole from him.

Securing the pole against the tree, she rose to her feet. David realizing she had stood, quickly jumped to his feet. She smiled as she wrapped the fish in some green leaves, securing them with some twigs. She invited him home for dinner and he accompanied her. He didn't realize they were at her parents' home until her father spoke.

Embarrassed and not knowing where he was, David turned to leave but Annitta smiled and guided him into her home and introduced him to her parents.

Two weeks later David and Annitta were married. The courtship was so quick and fast that David didn't know what was going one. He rarely said anything and he didn't mind because he liked the way she talked and he was no longer lonely. And over the years David became the proud father of seven sons and one daughter.

By the time the summer celebration drew nearer the animals were so nervous that some of them were sick, jumpy irritable and edgy. No effort was put into the parade and there were no floats, clowns or bands. The animals dressed in costumes and walked down the road to the clearing.

Saul came to the conclusion that he would never defeat David no matter what he did. So after the procession, he took to the podium to make an announcement. The animals groaned loudly. Instead of challenging David as he did in the past, he challenged the animals of same age to race against each other. The animals stood with their mouths wide open. They knew that their king was up to his tricks once again and, they as always would pay the price.

Many of the families were struggling to make a living because their husbands and sons were in prison. Because of the yearly festival, those in prison were released to be with their families. Afterward, they would return to the overcrowded jail.

Being apprehensive, the parents refused to allow their children to race. They had suffered enough and they were beyond caring what their king would do to them. The lives they were living were a prison without bars.

Saul sensing their hesitation began apologizing to the animals and explaining that this year and the years to come there would be no more foot races against him and David. This year he would race against his own species, the hares.

The animals still did not trust their king but they allowed their children to race. Once the race was over between the king and the hares, they breathed a sigh of relief. Saul, of course won the race.

After the races the musicians gathered up their instruments and began to play. For the first time in years the animals felt like dancing and dance they did. It was well into the evening before they were too tired to dance anymore.

Saul was oblivious to what was going on. His attention was focused on Thelma Beaver. He watched with longing as she danced with several of the young men. When the fourth song was played, she went and sat with her mother. He knew it was now or never as he walked over to her and asked her to dance. At first she was hesitant, looking at him with a frown on her face, then she smiled and took the hand he offered.

After the dance they went for a long walk and talked about many things but nothing important. Afterward, Saul invited her and her family to the palace for dinner. She accepted.

After a month of attending dinners and outings with the king, Thelma's family along with other dignitaries were invited to the castle. There was food, dancing and the animals had a grand time. This was the first time any of the animals had been invited to the castle since Saul became king.

As the clock struck midnight, Saul announced that Thelma Beaver had consented to become his wife and they were all invited to the wedding.

Never before in history had an animal dared to marry anyone outside his own species. Privately Thelma's father was appalled that the king would announce the engagement of his daughter without consulting with him. Even if the king had asked for his daughter's hand in marriage he would have given his consent. He felt that it was wrong for a beaver and a hare to marriage. This sort of thing did not happen.

Mr. Beaver tried to get an audience with the king, but he was barred from seeing the king. This infuriated him more. His wife just looked at him and smiled. She never once voiced her opinion regarding the marriage. She felt that if their daughter was happy with the arrangement, she had no objection to the marriage.

Mr. Beaver was furious about the arrangement and voiced his objections to some of his neighbors and friends, vowing that his daughter would not marry the king. His friends and neighbors were so angry at his decision that it almost caused a riot. They felt that if he did not allow his daughter to marry the king, he might impose more laws or worse of all, have him imprisoned. Mr. Beaver never thought of that and stopped his protest, but he was not happy.

After the marriage they had hoped that their lives would return to when King John reigned, but it didn't. The king didn't reduce the taxes nor did he decrease the size of the army but he rescinded many of the other laws. As a wedding present to the animals, Saul released many of the prisoners and they were able to reclaim their land but for the next seven years, they had to give half of their crops to the king. Those that had committed serious crimes were not released from jail. This was not what the animals had wished for, but they were happy just the same.

A month later the king and Thelma exchanged vows and she became the new queen. In honor of their marriage, the king summoned all the animals in the kingdom to witness their vows.

All the animals participated in the celebration with all their might, dancing, signing and playing all kinds of musical instruments – lyres, harps, tambourines, cymbals, and trumpets. It was a celebration fit for a king and queen. Not since the death of King John had the animals had such a wonderful time as they danced at the wedding of King Saul Hare and Queen Thelma Hare.

"The end," grandfather said looking over at the sleeping child.

He chucked to himself. He was twelve years old before he could stay awake to hear the end of the story. His grandson had several more years to go.

Rising from the chair, he went to the door. With his hand on the light switch, he turned and locked his gaze on his sleeping grandson and smiled. With one swoop, he cut off the light leaving the room in darkness. Only the moon and stars provided any light.

GOOD NIGHT!

Printed in the United States
17191LVS00003B/277-336